# A SCREAM in the SHADOWS

## Mac Donald Dixon

PAPILLOTE PRESS

London and Trafalgar, Dominica

First published by Papillote Press 2022 in Great Britain
© Mac Donald Dixon 2022

Printed and bound by CPI Group (UK) Ltd, Croydon CR0 4YY
Cover art by Marie Frederick
Book design by Andy Dark
Typeset in Minion
ISBN: 978-1-8380415-3-3
A CIP catalogue record for this book is available from the British Library.

Papillote Press
23 Rozel Road
London SW4 0EY
United Kingdom.
And Trafalgar, Dominica
www.papillotepress.co.uk

In memory of all women, and men, killed in the name of love, whose souls wander the earth seeking justice.

# Chapter
# 1

I was ten going on eleven when it happened. I remember brushing my teeth by the standpipe outside our house. It was early; I was cleaning myself for school, trying to remove bedding smells from my body and dreading the cold water that was about to fall on my skin. I hear my mother shout: "Andrew, hurry up an' bathe; don' forget you got school today." When she call me Andrew, I know things serious; most times is Andy when she want me to take this for her or find that. "Yes Mama!" I shout back straining my voice; it was not clear if she heard me or not. She did the same thing every morning from Monday to Friday once I reach under the standpipe and open the tap.

That day, out of the clear blue sky a thunder come rolling in from the sea. I look out to the east over the water and catch sight of a patch of black cloud. On the hill where we live, we had a clear view of the horizon in any season. I could hear Mama talking to my little brother Marvin, but her voice break in the strong wind that always come just before the rain. Mama dispatch Laurette, my big sister, she was two years older, to her seamstress, Miss Claire, who lived on the high road (she still lives there) near our school, to lengthen her school skirt.

Laurette was growing fast, Mama say. Big for thirteen and started wearing bra after she rush past twelve. Papa always get mad when fellas by the road whistle at her, especially in her school clothes. He had put two men in court for indecent assault, but I didn't know what that mean until I ask Mama and she

1

confuse me with her answer: "The boys touch Laurette where they not supposed to touch her." I was none the wiser. Laurette's uniform was riding up above her knee and she tell Mama the boys in her class were always looking under her skirt. She bathed early, long before me and take her tea. When I went out in the yard she was putting on her clothes. I see Papa in the kitchen when I just wake up and he was still there when Mama order me outside to bathe.

Laurette pass close by me while I naked under the standpipe. She throw a little stone in joke; it knock my backside, not hard, but I pretend to bawl. I feel her hand on my shoulder as she peep over and say softly, "You getting big boy!" I bar myself with both hands and, in the corner of my eye, watch her skip off down the little dirt road and disappear past Miss Philomene's house under the bush.

Mama send me by the seamstress later to ask if Laurette was still there. I couldn't see any good reason why I so close to my school that I must go back home just to tell Mama I didn't see Laurette, but if that is what Mama want, there is nothing I can do about it. I know Laurette sometimes stop and talk with Fafan when they meet in the gap. He was living at his grandmother Miss Philomene just below us. I didn't see anything in that, but I suspect Mama was suspicious and that's why she wanted me to report back. In fact, Miss Claire say that Laurette leave a long time ago — if I was drinking coffee it would get so cold I would have to throw it away. I reach to school just as it start, in time for prayers, let's say a little after nine o'clock.

Looking back over the years, I know I did not see Papa when I went back to the house. The last time I saw him (I am sure of this no matter what Mama say) was after Laurette hit me on my backside with the pebble. He leave home in a hurry, down the gap towards the high road; he was always in a rush. I recall him wearing khaki short pants, but no shirt. To me he had a white plastic bottle in his hand, but I am not sure. I don't know if it's my imagination playing tricks. I did not see him return; I would have been at school. But Mama claim he was in the kitchen when I left the house and even now, she sticks to this. She was certain I saw Papa eating a piece of bread and taking his tea while she watch me bathe. From the angle of the bath, it's not possible to see inside the kitchen. If I had seen him, I would remember saying goodbye to him when I leave for school but Mama does not want to hear that. In her mind, Papa was in the kitchen and never leave the house all morning until he go and help Miss Grainy cut a tree on her land above our house. Nobody can blame him for what happen outside, and I was her witness.

I find out about Laurette at school, a little before lunchtime. I was getting ready for prayers before meals, when a girl come in from the schoolyard screaming loud enough for everybody to hear: "They kill Laurette under the bush!"

The entire school down pencils and stop work. Teachers freeze at their blackboards with chalk in hand. The principal thought fast, rang the bell to bring us to order for grace although it was not quite on the hour. My eyes sweep across to where Laurette always sit in her class. She was absent. I wanted to shout out her name, but a foolish pride help me hush my mouth shut. That's not true, that's not true, I say to myself. I see Laurette just before I come to school; somebody playing a joke on us.

At twelve on the dot, lunchtime, school close. The undertaker had already come and park his hearse by the road. None of us remain in the schoolyard after that. They cover Laurette under a technicolour bed sheet; it was Mama's. I could see her shape through the cloth but not her face. Mama was leaning on Miss Philomene, who was holding her up. They were walking close behind the body. Mama had Marvin on her shoulder; he was too small for school.

Papa was leaning on the bonnet of the hearse talking to the driver; his eyes were dry. I could not hear the conversation, but I remember feeling cold when he see me. There was a large crowd, people I never see before looking on and saying their piece all at the same time. I didn't want to believe that it was my big sister under that sheet but when I get close I didn't dare lift it to find out. Children come up and speak to me. Don't ask me what they say. A girl offer me a piece of her bread, but I was not hungry. I didn't spend much time by the road but I remember going back to the schoolyard after I see my father and sit down under a tall guava tree that the children did not give a chance to bear ripe guavas and cry my head off, although I was not sure for what.

After school, I race home. When I finally get a chance to ask Mama what happen, she did not answer me straight. My mind strike a blank wall and everything inside it walked out of my head. When my father come home late that afternoon lamps were lit already. Mama said earlier, when I asked for him, that he take some fresh clothes and go with the hearse to Castries. It was so confusing; I cannot remember if I peed at all for the day.

Another thing I will never forget is that afternoon sitting by the table in the kitchen. Papa was not there; Mama just finish washing some glasses; people were coming to the house later. She was about to send me to Mr Paulinos for him to fill a white plastic gallon bottle with strong rum for her. His shop was lower down the high road on the same side as our gap. Mama was searching up and down for the bottle she always keep under the kitchen table. I tell her I saw Papa go down the road with a white plastic bottle that morning, but I also remember some days before he did mix Gramoxone in it to spray tomatoes. Mama always warning me that Gramoxone is a poison and I must never put it close to my mouth. I did not think that the white plastic bottle not being where it was supposed to be was strange, but Mama thought so and muttered loud enough for me to hear. I say to myself Papa know he mix poison in the bottle so he take it to throw away and forget to tell her.

From the very next day, with Laurette's body at the morgue in Castries, Mama start lecturing me on what to say to the police knowing they would come with questions after digesting the autopsy report. "Children does put their mother and father in trouble, so listen to me," she insist. "Say everything like I tell you to say it, like you say your prayers. Don' put your own two pence ha'penny in the sauce." Her face knot up; she was ready to put licks on me if I stutter. Mama begin sowing seeds in my mind, wild seeds, making me believe they were facts. She said they going to ask you the same questions until you get tired hearing them. "You must repeat the same answer each time, or else, you will trap yourself."

Why the police want to trap me? I had no knowledge of the law; my mind is not fully open up to life as yet. What does Mama mean? What did I do for me to trap myself? I'm not a bird that don't know glue. How she expect me to set a trap and get catch in it — with what? I was still a child, innocent and stupid when this thing happen. What they tell me to say I say and that made my mother happy.

I cannot change my statement now, even if I want to, and that's part of my problem with the system. Once you lie, you stick with it forever. If I say I want to correct my statement now that I know better, some smart lawyer will jump all over me and make a jury believe I am a liar. I don't know if what I said then help Papa and his case; it certainly does not look so to me. Things that did not have colour once — frying fish in oil without flour — start getting brown in their jackets, making me wonder why I couldn't see them like that before. Things I paid no mind to suddenly take on shapes, worms turn to butterflies, and mongoose make friends with fer-de-lance.

I can see Papa, boldface, trying to show me how he is so holy and innocent that a priest will give him communion without confession. After Laurette's death, he could not look at me or Mama in the eyes; it's something I never forget. Sometimes, I dream about him and I'm afraid to repeat what I see. Things come to me so real in my dreams I can touch them, and I could swear they always there. I feel afraid talking to myself and writing this down. When I mention my sister, my skin grow scales.

To me, then, it was a mystery how Laurette just stay so and die without falling sick though I hear at school that somebody kill her. The way Mama behave, I thought there was something more to it than just killing. Something I could not easily explain. Whatever it was seem bigger than me. It could have to do with the fight between God and the devil, which I been hearing about from the time I know myself. In the country, you learn to be more afraid of the dead than the living, and everything else you cannot understand is larger than life. For a long time, I believe Laurette's death had to do with evil spirits that roam about under the bush. Mama never fail to warn us be careful of strange sounds. "Not all the noise you hear during the day come from birds," she would say. "When you hear things you don' understand, go about your business as if you don' hear them."

At school, the children were whispering among themselves: "We know who kill Laurette! We know who kill Laurette!" When I tackle them, they afraid to tell me so I involve Mama. She shake her head and start crying. "Yes, maybe they know more than police; police don' know yet who do it."

"For what they kill her, Mama? Why the children saying they know who kill her?" She fly into a rage and demand I stop questioning her right away. "You not a lawyer. Wait when your time come to answer questions you don' go an' tell the police any stupidness an' put your father in trouble, ou tann, bon." Mama move between her own brand of English and Kwéyòl whenever she get vex and I inherit the habit from listening to her.

It don't matter how much I try hard to imagine Laurette was still alive, from the minute I see them push the stretcher into the back of the hearse, I know — only dead people go into the back of a hearse flat on their back. When it got closer to the funeral and the police release the corpse for burial, Mama break the news in her own strange way. One minute she looking at me, her mind far, and next, without looking, only her lips move to say, "We not going to be able to talk to Laurette again for a long time, but we will get a chance to see her before they plant her in the ground for good."

"When, Mama? Where?" I ask. Right away she start to cry again.

"She on the fridge in Castries, Lovence go an' see her already."

"Why Papa go without us?" I was curious. He knew all of us were anxious to see Laurette again so I couldn't understand why he would choose to go by himself.

"You don' ask big people their business!" Mama shout and shut me up with a slap.

Several days go by, each one taking longer to leave than the last, but news of Laurette's death refuse to get stale. It was the only hot rumour in Bwa Nèf and beyond. At the time, Bwa Nèf was a sleepy village on a hillside overlooking the sea on the east coast. The main road pass through it winding up hill like a corkscrew until you reach Tèt Chimen. Lower down, a narrow side road take you to the church and cemetery with the presbytery and schoolhouse nearby. The little wooden houses with their galvanise roofs, some older ones with shingles, pop up between the bushes every hundred yards or so on either side. There had never been anything as serious as a murder at Bwa Nèf and the people were afraid of police. They did not want them coming to their village and start locking them up on suspicion, like they hear happening in other parts of the island where poor people live.

People travel from as far away as Dennery village to come and see where Laurette's body was found and ask questions. Everybody say it was impossible to find her that quick except if you know where to look. They assume, 'Only the person who kill her would know where they hide the body.' It was a lonely part of the bush, near the river. How Laurette get there if somebody didn't carry her or was trying to hide her I don't know. No road will take you straight there and no young girl going there alone unless she got a good reason. Even I was afraid to pass there in the middle of the morning with other boys, the place dig deep into the bottom of the hill. Quiet, strange, dark, cold, the wind freezing your skin even when sun high up in the sky. The kind of place Mama would say you bound to get ladjablès. If I know my sister, no way she going there by herself. People come home to tell Mama about what they hear and she put on a bold face. Then she repeat what they say to Papa, and he storm out the house.

Out of the blue a few days after Laurette's death, Mama tell me that the police want to ask me some questions. They came to the house; it was a Saturday morning. All I could tell them was I never set eyes on Laurette again after she hit me with the little stone while I was bathing. I was in school when Papa find her. Don't remember if I cry, but I felt sad. I told them I would miss her when I was not in school and, until she come back, from this dying business, I will not be myself again. She did all the housework — carrying water, washing dishes, our clothes, sweeping out the house and putting Marvin to sleep. I had nothing to do on afternoons except play.

They take me in the front room, alone, while another detective stay with Mama in the kitchen. A woman from social services, who the police tell me was a lawyer sit by me, while two big men corner me in the old Morris chair. I wanted to show the detectives that I was Mama's little innocent boy boasting that boys don't do housework, that's for girls to do. I believed that, deep down, after seeing my father strut around the house doing nothing while Mama work her tail off in the kitchen. Boys learn to make garden with their fathers; look after sheep and goats in the pasture and feed the cow. I wanted the detectives to know Mama was a good person. How could a good person have anything to do with the death of her own child?

My father was not interested in what was happening in the house with us. Bringing up children was Mama's job. He was quiet, and you never know when he in the house until he come in the kitchen to eat. The most he do was a little garden behind the kitchen and a day's job here and there when he could find work. When Papa feel like bathing in the river, if no school, he would take me with him and show me how to catch crayfish with my bare hands and make traps for birds. My mind was still on church and God and first communion, bad things did not enter my head; I wasn't holy-holy, never was an acolyte, or anything like that. I say my prayers first thing on mornings before I pass water in my mouth and last thing at night before I close my eyes.

No way I could think Papa was evil; he did not look like a person who would do bad things. But then what can we tell by a person's looks? However, looking back, I know enough to know my father was not a man to take for granted although I don't remember him ever raising his hand on either me or Laurette. That job was Mama's. The most he would do if we make too much noise is shout "Mama" and she came right away to put peace. Sometimes I wonder if I really know my father. I don't think as a child there was ever a serious conversation between us, except on days by the river, but then I did most of the talking. He was seldom home long enough to teach me to lace my shoes or send me on errands.

I wake up from sleep in the dark soaking wet searching for Laurette using my hands. She sleep by herself in a corner on her own little pile of bedding, to beg her find an old dress for me, one she or my mother was not wearing again. I needed a dry old dress to put on; sleep never take me in wet clothes not even if I dry myself and stay naked. I call her name, soft, didn't want to wake Mama — then I remember, Laurette was no longer here with us. Mama would sleep hard after she drain her tears, my little brother Marvin on the bed next to her — he sleeps with her when Papa not around — they could not hear the wind even if it tear the old galvanise roof off the house. How long I stay awake taking off wet clothes and falling back naked on the floor, I don't know. It took many, many years for me to catch myself again.

Last time I saw Laurette was in the cemetery before they screw the lid on her coffin. She had on lipstick for the first time and a strange smile across her lips. I thought she spoke to me with her eyes closed but was too frightened to understand what she said. Not until I see men in the graveyard shovelling dirt on her coffin that I agree, halfway at least, maybe she die in truth, but still not fully understanding the consequences of death. I know I would not see her again for a long, long time. How she would manage alone, by herself, under all that pile of dirt was beyond me.

I never realise I remembered so much about Laurette's funeral until I was much older. That afternoon, through my damp eyes, I was standing on the church steps holding Mama's hand. Papa was right behind us, hiding, smoking a cigarette. Our cousin Miss Eldra and her youngest daughter, who was standing next to Mama, had Marvin on her shoulder fast asleep. I hear Miss Eldra chastise Papa and ask him to out the cigarette when the hearse arrive. Some older boys from the school take charge of the coffin when the driver open the back of the hearse. They climb the steps and stop at the entrance, the priest and acolytes come down with the cross, say some prayers and the boys carry the coffin up the aisle behind him.

Mama, me, Miss Eldra, her daughter with Marvin, follow behind the coffin. But not Papa, he stay outside with his friends. We sit down in a pew up front. The boys place Laurette's coffin on a bier and went to sing with the school choir. Mama crying on Miss Eldra's shoulder send me fighting back tears. I find it strange Papa did not come and sit with us and I keep looking back to see if he came inside but the church was so fill I couldn't see past the pew behind us.

People come from everywhere, from as far as Castries, dressed in their Sunday best smelling of all kinds of perfume I never smell before until that afternoon. There were many speakers. I can't remember anything that was said but when the priest began smoking the coffin, I couldn't take the smell of the incense and my head went light. The next thing was the crowd in the cemetery begging Mama to open the coffin for them to see Laurette for the last. Neither Mama nor Papa had time for me that afternoon. Mama was busy talking to people she didn't know; some brought wreaths, some handed her sympathy cards in white envelopes. Papa was making himself busy with the gravediggers, belching smoke through his nose like he was a chimney.

Fore-day morning, six months after Laurette's funeral. Cocks were crowing loud in the yard; I turn a little on my side to ease out of the dream to hear like somebody knocking hard on the door. I was tempted to get up and check, but something tell me go back to sleep. Next, I wake up for good to a loud banging. Men shouting: "Open! Police!" Mama get up, shaking Papa; he was a hard sleeper. "Wake up, Lovence, police!" Papa yawn but quickly catch himself and put on his pants. I follow them to the door. Marvin was still asleep. Four officers in plainclothes rush inside as soon as Papa turn the key in the lock. One of them had a sheet of paper in his hand. "Are you Lovence St Mark?"

"What?" Papa look stunned, he couldn't say much.

"What happen to Lovence St Mark? Yes, is his house…" Mama was ready to take on all four officers.

"This is your husband?" The officer with the paper ask.

"Yes, is Lovence."

"Lovence St Mark, I have a warrant for your arrest for the murder of Laurette Stephen. From now on anything you say can be taken down and held in evidence against you."

An officer took out a pair of handcuffs and secure Lovence St Mark's hands behind his back. Mama went cold. I follow Papa when the police march him outside. There were six in all, two armed with rifles stayed outside; Mama try to hold me back in the doorway, but I slip through her hands.

Although still very early, a crowd gathered by the road. Children were there with their parents and later in school they were happy to tell me how the police manhandled Papa and shove him into the back of their jeep. It was not a good day for me. At school I hang my head in shame over my desk listening to the children speak about my father. They didn't care if I got vex; they were with one voice: "The police walk him from his house, push him in the back seat an' carry him down to the station, bouwo-a," they rejoiced.

The news went wild, swinging on vines around Bwa Nèf, uphill to Tèt Chimen and deep into Gwan Bwa. Papa was arrested and condemned without a hearing or a trial and his whole family crucified in the process. In this little place behind God's back, justice is one face you seldom see, and if you poor, you might never see it. Sometimes, time sits on your case and after several years will allow you a hearing. By then you would be lucky if witnesses remember your face. For my father it would be many years before his day came.

To say I remember Papa ever speak to me the morning police come for him, either in sympathy, pity or regret, would be a lie. He keep his face in front and didn't look back. One of our cousins, Miss Eldra's eldest daughter from Tèt Chimen, come by the school to collect me that afternoon and take me to her house. She was on her own living with her boyfriend. I stay with her because Mama went with Marvin to Dennery Police Station where they charge Papa without bail. Nobody could explain that to me and I did not understand what was going on. Who so stupid to believe Papa will kill his own child? You only kill your enemies, people who hurt you, those that do things to send you to the mad house, or worse, those that use obeah to destroy you.

However, I understood if you don't believe in obeah, you safe. Couldn't say I was safe, I had my own beliefs growing up in a house where good and evil speak from the same side of your mouth. Living in the country you learn to kill cockroach, rats, bugs, lots of birds and snakes, a fowl for first communion and Christmas, even manicou, but not people. "Thou shalt not kill" is in your face every day, from mother, teacher, and priest.

I hear a lot of things at school when Mama could afford to send me. The older girls, Laurette's friends, said I would grow up to be just like my father. Mama threaten to come to the school to report them to the head teacher, but never did. Life get harder for us, and Mama seldom had money to buy lunch. It was only when she get a little work with Miss Grainy peeling spice, cleaning nutmegs and collecting mace that she would have small change to buy bread and a tin of sardines for me and Marvin to share during lunch break. She did not have to cook for twelve o'clock; Papa was not around to suddenly appear pretending he was hungry on days when nobody at Paulinos' bar was buying him drinks.

Mama paid more attention to Papa than to us. She always find money wherever it was, from relatives or friends, to buy food, clothes, to take to Castries when she visit Papa in custody. Being the older brother, I had to teach Marvin how to fend for himself. Most days we ate whatever fruit was in season, fished for eels in the river which we cook sometimes without salt and collect ground provisions from our cousins at Tèt Chimen. I felt ashamed not being able to take care of the family during Papa's absence — he never come back until I was grown up and living in my own house — but could not let my little brother see.

I try hard to forget that Papa was in prison all those ye
it still plays on my mind. Mama's visits to Castries, up and
like a donkey on the high road while Papa remain locked up
not easy to understand either, especially not knowing when P
would be released. That was the worst of all; it would hit me har
Mama never stop crying at nights pouring her grief out to her
pillow, repeating Papa's name, missing her man more than she
ever miss us. You'd swear we were nowhere around. If we dare
ask her what was wrong, the huff she would let out was louder
than any scream she make; so loud you would hear her voice all
the way down in the village.

She pretend to neighbours who call to bring yams, or
breadfruits when in season, that she no longer care about herself,
no man would look at her again twice if anything happened to
Lovence. The neighbours didn't have to ask questions, she
volunteered, and she did not hesitate to blame her children for
her apparent self-neglect; one was dead, but she still blamed all
three and detested the police for keeping her husband in custody.
"Without asking questions, without taking him to court, because
they say (stressing on the they) is he kill Laurette."

Mama make it a habit of repeating how Papa take all his money
and give to lawyers who fool him so there is nothing left to spend
on us. That would be fair had it been true but Papa had no money
in the first place. His lawyers were all court appointed, and some
young ones worked pro bono hoping to make their name. I could
not understand how Papa was accused of murdering Laurette
and nobody, except for the children at school, could say how he
manage to do it. There were rumours out of Mr Paulinos' rum
shop that Laurette was strangled; there were stories she might
have been raped, but the men spoke soft whenever they saw me
coming on errands. Nevertheless, not a soul on God's earth could

this. The man couldn't kill a cockroach ... life.

...he story than I was being told. My little ... overtime and I begin asking myself ... Mama insist on me telling the police I see Papa ...en when I leave for school? I could not say he was; I ...xed up between what I thought I saw and what she wanted ... to believe. Who set police on Papa was the question on my mind: a neighbour, somebody with a grudge, or the real murderer? Why so many things remain above my head, things I cannot understand? I needed answers but did not know where to go to find them.

# Chapter
# 2

Three years after Laurette's death I passed the Common Entrance exam and went to Dennery Secondary School. My mother arranged with my nennenn in the village for me to stay with her on weekdays and come home on weekends. This give me a fresh start; life got easier with less hassle and I made a new set of friends. I saw my old friends sometimes when I visited Mama and Marvin, but they no longer had any interest in me. Nobody at my new school seem to know anything about my father, or what happen to Laurette. Everybody was about their own business and didn't care. I spent the happiest five years of school life in Dennery and not until after I left realised they were.

It was at school in Dennery that the thought came to me to join the police force. My mother's visits to Castries still troubled me. Unless something drastic was done, Papa would rot in jail — that much I was convinced.

Somewhere around third form I drowned myself in schoolwork and with help from my godmother, a retired primary school principal who drill me in English and Math — my two weakest subjects. I graduate in form five with a CXC certificate in six subjects. On leaving school, without consulting anyone, I applied to join the Royal St Lucia Police Force. Unlike my schoolfellows, who sent out applications to government and some of the large stores in Castries, I only applied one place. I made up my mind that becoming a policeman was the only way I could help Papa. Nothing seem to be happening with his case and my mother was getting thinner and thinner with worries.

The Police Chief called me for an interview. I was successful and spent six months at training school learning everything from basic policing to weaponry, then another six months on the beat around Castries. As a young police officer, my eyes began to open on the world. I was interested in everything, like my mother would say, in what don't concern me. I hear and see things you will not believe happening every day in this little country — the innocent getting paid to plead guilty for big shots; offenders bribing their way out of trouble and those whose only crime was being in the wrong place at the wrong time going to jail to settle the crimes of their rich pardners. It's a society that don't give a damn about the poor anyway. Once there is money to pass around, it's guaranteed that the boss man or big-shot son like on TV will find himself on a direct flight to New York after his family bandy together to make bail and pay for the economy ticket to get him out. While a poor boy, possibly innocent, is held forever for questioning because he cannot afford a lawyer.

During my first six months on the beat, Papa had been on remand for more than nine years; nine months would be long enough in any other matter. I was down for guard duty on the opening day of October assizes when I saw my father's name on the case list. There was no way I wanted Papa to see me in uniform, with a gun strapped by my side, especially if I was to guard him. Worst yet, for me to be the one to unlock his handcuffs in court. While I carried the same surname like my father, nobody in the police force made the connection. When I decided to tell my sergeant, he looked shocked for days. "When we discussing the case between us, you does stay there listening and say nothing." That was the most he could manage and apologised for anything he might have said about Papa contrary to presuming his innocence until proven guilty. "We talk a lot of crap between us, but we don't always follow what we say."

I told him, "No hard feelings. We call that venting from shock or frustration." He admit sometimes he was hasty and allow his suspicions to show on his sleeves and I had every right to get vex if I did. "You could choose your friends, but you can't choose your family," he acknowledged, and reassign me to beat duty that day far from the courthouse.

After I completed the course to become a detective and pass the exams, I was transferred almost immediately to CID at police headquarters. There I encountered Sergeant Willius. It turn out he was from Praslin, a fishing village on the east coast where I had heard Papa and Mama come from. When I tell him who I was, he pretend not to believe me until I start repeating names from my entire generation, those I know and others I remember from listening to Mama. Then he said he knew my mother well; she was a distant cousin.

What he say next come to me like a shock. I learn that Mama had a child already when she meet Papa — a little girl. It was Laurette, her first child. Sergeant Willius remember her as a baby on Mama's shoulders: "Always smiling, she had nice eyes, a loving baby girl," he said.

I grow up in the house never knowing Papa was not Laurette's natural father — he did not show her a different face to us as far as I know. Why Mama never thought she should tell us the truth, I will not understand. Home affairs should not be a secret; there is no shame in having a child before marriage even if the man you finally marry is not the child's father. My suspicious mind tell me there were other reasons Mama never tell us. Maybe she didn't want me looking at Laurette as if she was not my sister. I could understand holding back the truth from Marvin until he was old enough, but not from me or Laurette. That's if Laurette ever know who was her real father.

My gut reaction was to hate Sergeant Willius for shocking me with this news, but I couldn't. He took a big brother approach to me from the day I landed in his department — before he knew we were relatives. I thought of confronting Mama but feared her outbursts. I know how emotional she could be about things that involve Papa so it was best to let "sleeping dogs lie".

Sergeant Willius insist it was important for me to know certain things. "Your father at Praslin was a big-time sagaboy. He take your mother and Laurette away from the village to live with him at Bwa Nèf, far away from people they know because he was afraid Agnes would make back with her child father."

"My father was jealous?"

"I don't think Agnes family ever like him for her."

"Somehow, you not describing the same man Mama say is my father," I said, laughing. He gave me a look and I braced myself to hear more. "Her father never wanted him for her. He called him 'the flashy man, fresh from cutting cane in the States'. Every time he remember Lovence he would shake his head. I knew Lovence, always swanking in his black-and-white leather shoes, fancy clothes, gold teeth in his mouth and nothing in his pocket. He sweep Agnes off her feet with fancy talk and take her away from her family."

"Gold teeth, yes, flashy, no. That's two different people." Sarge sent my mind into overdrive. "That's not the Lovence St Mark I know."

"By the time you get to know him he had cool down. He had responsibility, a wife and children. Your mother was a good-looking chick." I sense a bit of envy in his voice trying to picture Mama in his mind. "Her father wanted her to go to Castries and educate herself to be a nurse — that and housemaid job was the only work a young woman from the country could get in those days. Don't forget she was not married and had one child already."

Sarge change the conversation — back to police work. Maybe he feel he was stretching too far. "You should switch your focus from current affairs to cold case files. From the way you look at things I can see you got natural aptitude for that side of the job." He said I was patient with a good memory. My colleagues praise me for being observant.

My body itch for the day when I could open Papa's dossier and read details for myself. This gave me motivation to approach my new assignment. I start going through the cold case files under Sarge's supervision, making observations that should have been clear from the beginning. Yet I could not escape opposition from a group of senior detectives whenever I uncover these matters, and it was much worse when I ask questions about Papa's case. They blocked me at every turn using every trick from their years of experience.

A corporal, who claim he worked on Papa's case from day one, always seemed offended when I limed around his workstation. He told me frankly I was digging my nose in an old sore foot and would only make things worse for myself. The man was counting his days to retirement reporting to work and doing the bare minimum. (I want to recall his face among the plainclothes policemen from Vieux Fort station who arrested Papa that early morning.) Sarge said the corporal became frustrated when he was overlooked for promotion and would take it out on suspects. The corporal had a reputation for beating men with electric cord wire on the soles of their feet without leaving any marks. I became suspicious after hearing this, if as he claim, he work on

Papa's case from the beginning. Maybe, just maybe, he could be the culprit responsible for the case not being called.

Sarge told me there was an old trick among senior detectives. Those in line for promotion, days before the chief made the announcements, would arrest a bunch of suspects on incomplete evidence to enhance their CVs. Sarge said the corporal was the last survivor of that dying breed. I resented the man, but Sarge warned me against acting on impulses. "He has a small following among other senior detectives, who believe in his methods. They use him whenever there is a tough nut to crack. The chief knows of his reputation but turns a blind eye because he produces results."

"What next?" I shrug in disgust and move on.

Like an eye over my shoulders, the corporal and his gang worm their way into almost every review I tackle. They insist I report to them because they know the history of everything in the files. The corporal appointed himself my immediate supervisor and informed me at every opportunity on the effectiveness of his methods, measured by the number of convictions he secured every week. They did not like seeing me in the company of Sergeant Willius and said to my face that I was sucking up to him for promotion. "That will never happen once I still on the force," the corporal told me one night while I was by myself in the canteen mulling over a hard day, and I believe him. He complain to Sergeant Willius about me, and swear blind I was digging into matters that did not concern me.

The divisions in the department affected morale. Older detectives supported the maverick corporal while younger ones like me sided with Sarge. It was difficult to notice this from outside looking in, but the slow pace of detection along with the length of time it took from arrest to trial spoke volumes. Then there was malice aimed at me: like the day somebody pour salt in a flask of coffee on my desk. Or when a smart jackass paint cow-itch all over the cushion on my chair that send me up and down like a jumping jack much to the silent enjoyment of the senior squad who made sure they were all at ringside to celebrate. Snitchers are not welcome and I suffered all these indignities without telling Sarge no matter how depressed I felt.

Corporal has since passed so I will not mention him by name out of respect for his children, two of them are now police officers. Sarge never bother me about the corporal's complaints about me until much later, long after he died. All his complaints were based on my being nosey and, as Laurette's brother, too close to be objective. When I get to know this, I redouble my efforts, delving into every matter he had personally handled. I found quite a few cases where people pleaded guilty without supporting evidence. When I referred the files to Sarge, he ask me to label them: "Guilty on suspicion of committing a crime." As if there was such a thing in law.

I went through some of the toughest times during those early years as a detective and in the end it only serve to harden me on the job. I don't know if it was the resentment coming from certain quarters, or the selective pile of unsolvable cases thrown on my desk by my corporal friend hoping I give up and resign in disgust. Instead, I became a man on a mission, I intended to do well, and nothing would stop me. Now that everyone in the squad knew I was Lovence St Mark's son I could not be assigned to the case. Besides, it was not marked as a cold case. I relied on Sergeant Willius to give me permission every time I wanted to take a peep at Papa's dossier. Unofficially, I was trying to reopen the investigation to find new evidence that could acquit him. I hoped to find uncorroborated evidence, even plausible suspects to give Papa some measure of reasonable doubt to get out of prison.

Every spare moment I spend reading files had to do with Papa's case. No one, apart from Sergeant Willius, knew my plans. It took more than planning to escape detection and I ran the risk of being caught with files on my desk whether I have permission to review them or not. Not having a working photocopier in the department made matters worse.

Many open confrontations between Sarge and the corporal were on account of science against supposition, as Sarge called it. He was open-minded, from the new school of law men, younger officers swore by him because he allowed them full range to develop their theories and to use scientific methods to improve their powers of detection. Fingerprinting was supported with DNA, and blood evidence moved from type comparison to more intricate analysis, which involved dextrose, nitrogen, and phosphate markers. However, all this was happening at the expense of good old policing legwork that take suspects through crime scenes until they stumble over themselves and confess. The older cops lamented the death of the old ways although there was no order from above demanding that they discontinue them. They felt a real threat was ignored in favour of high-tech gadgets that cost the unit an arm and a leg. Men like Sergeant Willius and other younger officers took the brunt of their rage and junior policemen like me suffered from their wrath, mixed with ample doses of jealousy and scorn. The police force was in transit, change was coming but a slow pace because the old guard still held on to power in the other divisions, particularly outside the capital where a corporal was still king and could sweat out any private under his supervision.

However, Sergeant Willius was not going to send me anywhere close to those bulldogs who were filing their teeth waiting for the day when I reported to work at their outposts. Once he was in charge at CID, I was safe.

The plot feels a bit elementary. I don't think I need to advance to read this

# Chapter
## 3

My father's case was called every year, at least once, sometimes twice, but on account of some technicality it was always adjourned. So back he went to Her Majesty's Prison in Castries, to an overcrowded jail full of inmates awaiting trial, mostly young men, underprivileged, with no job. Papa's lawyers were having a ball drawing fees from government without having to work. For eleven years Mama went up and down the road hoping for a trial, but there was only adjournment after adjournment — world without end, but no amen. Detectives who started as juniors on the case got promoted; some left the force. The Chief of Police job changed hands umpteen times, lawyers came, and lawyers went. Every time they take my father to court, they started afresh like it was a new case. Everyone was green except the accused. One day when I couldn't take it again, feeling sorry for Mama, I ask Sergeant Willius, boldface, "What you think going on with Papa's matter?"

"What you mean?" he grinned, taken by surprise.

"You think he guilty?" I pressed him.

"I'm not a judge, I'm not the jury."

"Things look too neat," I stammered. "It so easy to plant evidence."

"Ah! That's good, an open mind, keep an open mind," was all he said. However, after remaining silent for a while, he swallowed his spit and spoke. "I was a little policeman when this commotion started. I know your mother long; we grow up together. She was damn good-looking when she was young. If we were not family, I could have married her. I find myself on the case when I get to know her husband was involved. My spirit never take to him, but like I tell you, always approach the case with an open mind." Questions came racing through my head. Suddenly, I wanted to know more than there was to know about and beyond this case.

"The files are there for you to go through when you want," Sarge said. "You got a lot of reading to do to catch up."

"You will help me?" I teased. Once Sarge is in my corner I will reach where I want to go.

"I too have a lot of questions. One thing though, don't involve the others. Keep whatever you find between us."

"You don't have to tell me, Sarge."

Before this it was glimpses, now I was getting the access I needed, although still supervised. Sarge gave me permission to move into second gear. It was either I prove my father innocent, like I believe he was, by identifying the real killer, or face the music. I was bias as expected. After all, it was my father who was accused. Laurette was my sister; we live in the same house with him. Nobody could convince me that Papa had the heart to kill her. There must be somebody else involved. Somebody in the files, like a dark shadow, waiting for me to uncover.

I start visiting my mother again; I had stopped for about three years; I couldn't take the crying. Marvin was at school weekdays, or out liming with friends on weekends, and I suspect she was lonely without Papa.

One of the first things I did at Bwa Nèf was to visit the site where Laurette's body was found. As a child, I had seen pictures of the spot. Papa brought home a newspaper and I recognised it by the big stone the women would hide behind to change their clothes after taking a dip in the basen a little higher up from where they washed in the river currents on Monday mornings. I had been down to the river many times with Papa to bathe and to catch kwibich. One track takes you there from wherever you start, no matter on which side of the river. It was a skimpy footpath linked to the dirt road to our house, a short cut they say that end at Tèt Chimen. But this was not a trail for children to follow unless in a group. Besides, it was longer than following the main road. However, there were many trees to provide shade making it cooler than the hot pitch any time of day. The whole place look like somebody put a curse on it. From police files I learn that Papa find Laurette's body behind the big stone by the river under some fat-poke trees that hide the women from people spying down on them from the hill.

That day the river water was crystal just as I remembered it from childhood. There had been no heavy rains for a couple of days. The place was desolate, with a heaviness in the air that had me sweating like the old blacksmith on Dennery main street. It was chilly, although the sun was shining, and I could hear the birds singing as they hop from branch to branch above my head. So many memories. My head was spinning nonsense, the kind I use to hear growing up, like Laurette was sold to the devil and he come for her on a morning that was not a saint's day. Who sold her nobody knew, but standing on the riverbank gazing at the spot where I believe she breathe her last, one question come to me: how it was possible to find her so fast lying in that hole? That question does not have an easy answer. Somebody had to know she was there.

On another visit, I find myself following the track to Miss Claire's house. She was one of the last persons to see Laurette alive. I thought, perhaps, she could tell me a lot. Miss Claire's house stands by itself on the main road, a small incline from where you can see the church at the back, between the presbytery and the belfry; the belfry is by itself, a little away off facing the entrance to the cemetery. You can also see the schoolhouse from there. If I could remember exactly where my sister was buried, I would have visited her grave first before going in by Miss Claire, but I could not. I peep through the old broken-down wooden gate, but all the graves look alike with their black crosses and white letters beaten by rain which falls often up here, close to the clouds. A green carpet cover the ground from corner to corner, spotted with wild yellow flowers in between. I could see all this, but nothing to direct me to where Laurette lay in the ground.

Miss Claire didn't know me well while I was growing up like she knew Laurette. She last see me as a child and did not recognise the big man knocking down her door. My face had changed from the little manicou schoolboy with grinning teeth, into a big thick man with broad shoulders.

After Laurette died, I don't remember having to go back to Miss Claire house for anything. My mother went herself; she didn't want me interfering in women's affairs, things like her dress and petticoat and other clothes were not for me to handle. She repeat on several occasions, life was bad enough as it was, she couldn't afford any of her boys turning makoumé on top of everything else — whatever she meant. I was clueless. However, I don't think she was serious. Mama was seldom careful with her tongue and said things that hurt innocent people. Miss Claire sew for her on credit until she found something to do to pay her. This was perhaps the real reason she would go herself, to spare us the embarrassment of begging. She was very proud in her own little way.

When I introduce myself, Miss Claire's eyes light up. She jump up from behind her sewing machine to come across to hug and kiss me — something I believe she never do before — she was stitching together a skirt and left it under the needle. She make it look like I was her long-lost prodigal son returning from London for Christmas after not writing for the whole eleven years I gone. "Little boy I see coming here to make message for your mother, you so big man already?"

She take a step back to size me up, her measuring tape hanging loose around her neck like a scapular. Shabin complexion, short, no more than five feet, stout with beady eyes, her reading glasses for threading needles down on her nose bridge. "Like is only yesterday morning I see Laurette take your hand, helping to make you cross the road. Always quiet, by yourself. You never have a lot of friends behind you." Her face turn serious while she size me up. "You see what your father cause; see the blight he put on this nice little place? Not even wood you can find to make coals nowadays." She made a quick sign of the cross, blessing herself and straightening her skirt around her broad waist before asking me about my mother. "Long time I don' see her."

She inquire if Mama was sick, or, if she was still frighten to go out alone. "You know how people stand nowadays," she said looking at me, trying to show sympathy. I was not convinced. I just came from Castries and was catching my breath before I go by my mother, so her nice little words went past me.

Miss Claire did not wait for an answer, she switch to another set of questions, which she seem she more eager to ask: "You must be full of girlfriends. You married? You got children yet?" I smile; I didn't think it her business to know I had a child on the way. I came close to telling her about Angel, my girlfriend, but decided to wait until the excitement of seeing me again leave her system. However, it was time to tell her my real reason for stopping by her house. I mention casually I would see Mama when she came to Castries. "The last time she came was when they call Papa's case about a year ago. That's why I start coming up here again."

"Your mother is your mother, boy. Don' care what happen, you must make time to see her."

"Yes, Miss Claire!" I said. I had to be careful not to mention my job. If she knew for sure, she would clamp shut on me like all the other country people once I start asking questions. I don't know why they hate to talk to the law; maybe they are afraid of looking stupid or sounding out of place.

The way Miss Claire look at me over her glasses, I think she was marking time to reprimand me for not visiting her more often. I feel apprehensive when it came to questioning her but I come straight to the point. "You can still remember the last time you see Laurette?"

"Of course, yes," she replied. "I remember, I remember a lot of things." There was a pinch of suspicion in her voice, maybe it was just me and my police mind. I calm down my fears swallowing my spit, a habit I copy from Sarge.

"I remember the morning she come an' bring her uniform for me to hem in a black plastic bag." Miss Claire did not need prompting. "She sit down in the corner over there." Miss Claire pointed to the corner opposite her sewing machine. "The same chair there still in the same place up to now; she was a nice child, good manners. God doesn't let his little angels stay long with us devils," she giggled. The way she did it I thought Miss Claire was about to cry, but her eyes were dry.

"Her little face follow my hand with the needle watching me how I make the stitches, up an' down, like she self was sewing —

I always here where you find me, behind the machine. I stay looking at her, my hand working, she don' know I watching her. When I was her age, I had to learn to do a lot of things: sew, cook, wash, scrub, make garden, everything. My mother say we never know what kind of man we goin' to get so we have to be ready for anything that come. If you unlucky an' get a man that lazy, you know is you that have to feed him." She laugh shaking her body like a tree trunk in strong wind.

"How long did Laurette have to wait for her uniform?" I squeeze a question through.

"Five minutes, not more. I don' take long to stitch a hem, even when I use needle an' thread. That's one thing I can do fast an' well."

"You use the machine to hem her uniform that morning?"

"What it was again, a uniform or a skirt?" I could feel her thinking. "So much time pass I don' well remember. It was a skirt, I think, I had to make it longer, it was getting to be too short for her, riding up her legs. She was growing so fast, her mother tell me. I make her unstitch the old hem an' thread the needle for me. I remember now, it was her school uniform. I can hem that before you finish drinking a cup of coffee, an' I not talking about if it cold. When I finish, she tell me thanks an' ask me how much like she have money to pay me. She says her mother ask her to find out. I tell her don' worry where Agnes getting the money from to pay me if I have to charge her for everything I do for her. Laurette fold her uniform an' put it in the black plastic bag, get up from the chair an' out the door like a breeze."

"She say thanks an' ask me how much?" I shake my head repeating Miss Claire's words quietly while thinking of other questions that would not aggravate or get her suspicious.

"Of course, yes, Agnes teach all of you good manners, down to your last little brother." Miss Claire was assertive and quite pleased with herself.

"That's true," I said. "Mama always insist we show respect to older people, even those that was not her friends." I thought about what I had just said and images of Mama frame on my mind. "Always say good morning or good afternoon when you pass people on the road. You don't know where you will fall." I never understand her reasoning, but, as children, Laurette and I had to obey, or else.

Miss Claire was not through with me. Her eyelids close a little, squinting as she look through the open doorway: "She was in a hurry to go back home an' get ready for school. Children like her always early. I see her sometimes when she pass with her friends on a morning. Never late, just like me an' church. I rather come early an' sit down, say a novena an' wait for the priest. I don't go to mass if I know I late."

"You living so close to God, you can never be late." I try a joke and succeed in getting Miss Claire to giggle. Thinking she was relaxed, I ask: "You saw Laurette again that day? She had to pass back here to go to school."

"See who?" Miss Claire looked up to heaven, lines crisscross her forehead. I could not tell if she was sad or annoyed. "The only chance I get to see Laurette again is when the police and them bring her on the stretcher by the road. I stay right here and watch through the jalouzi. Too much people: police, detective, school children, everybody sticking in your foot, not me." She was reliving the day all over again. "The child just leave here to go to her house, next thing I hearing is they find her under the bush, dead. Without clothes, all her little self outside — I does feel a kind of way when I remember that. Up to now I does want to cry cause I seeing her looking at me stitching; just there." Her voice taper off.

This was exactly what I wanted, details. "How you get to know Laurette was dead?" I pause to repeat, then add: "Who told you?"

"Mr Lucius come here long before police reach. It didn't have people by the road yet."

"Who is Mr Lucius?" I did not remember seeing the name on the witness list.

"He ringing the bell in church. He is Merle father, my last child. He does get up early to ring the bell before he go an' look for his cow. You know Merle, she use to teach before she start making baby for that stupid man she go an' married after I warn her."

I come to say oh shoot but shut my mouth quick. "She teach me in ABC," I answered before Miss Claire trot off on a tangent. "Let's go back," I said. "Tell me about Mr Lucius and how he get involved?"

"Involve? Mr Lucius not involve in nothing!" She was on her high horse raising her voice to defend her child father. I apologise for creating the misunderstanding. "Wrong word. The English language is a cruel animal," I stammer half-hearted and we both laugh.

"He tell me Lovence meet him at Tèt Chimen coming down after he finish giving the animal water. Before he could say morning, Lovence tell him how he find Laurette dead under the bush, her mouth was wide open and full of foam, he take the smell of Gramoxone on her." That was important evidence — it was not in any file I read so far. Thank God for memory: Mama searching for the white plastic bottle she always keep under the kitchen table… Papa mix Gramoxone in it. Wow! Surely Mr Lucius had to be on file under another name. What he had to say too important to leave out. I remain quiet. I didn't want to set

Miss Claire off on the wrong foot again, but I needed to hear more about Mr Lucius.

"What time Mr Lucius come back from looking after his cow that morning?" Somewhere in the back of my mind timing would help me to solve this case. Somebody had to be in the bush waiting for Laurette between the time she was last seen crossing the road and when Papa came by the road to say he find her. The whole thing looked premeditated to me. Somebody was following her, whoever that is they got to be suspect number one.

"Lucius was here when the child come with her uniform. They speak. He ask her about her father; it had long he didn't see him." Miss Claire pause to remember. "Laurette was not dead yet. I want you to understand that well." She guarded her words as if protecting somebody.

"From the little I can gather so far Laurette was last seen crossing the road around eight that morning. I don't want to waste your time going over what happen while Laurette was still alive if it can't help me understand more about her death. You are very busy and have your housework to see about; I can't expect you'll waste precious time on me."

Miss Claire smiled. "You was a child, is for us old people to tell you. The truth don' always come out in court. Let me speak and don' stop me until I finish." Nothing can stop Miss Claire when she start. "Lucius was in the kitchen, he finish his coffee and get up to go when Laurette reach. I tell him if he find a yam or a bunch of macamboo, bring it when he coming, I had nothing to cook. A good few minutes after the child leave, he take his cutlass an' go up the road."

"You remember the time?"

"No!" She regretted that; I could see her looking sad.

"What time you see Mr Lucius again?"

"I can't tell you that either, I don't keep clock around here to give me pressure. But he come back straight away, right after he finish water his cow. Lovence did pass here already but didn't say anything. He stand up outside by the door" — Miss Claire point to the steps — "looking under my table, under my chairs as if he searching for something he lose. I ask him why he don' come in thinking is something he want me to sew for him an' was afraid to ask. He tell me, it alright. I could see his eyes working like torchlight digging in all corners so I ask him again. He bend his head, look at the floor but couldn't face me eye to eye. Agnes send him — so he say — to call Laurette; it was way past the time for school. He say something like he don' know what the child still doing here, not today her mother send her to hem her uniform an' she can't reach back home yet."

The question I dread to ask come to mind, "What time was that?" Miss Claire get vex; I was upsetting her with this time thing. If I can only get her to understand I trying to establish who was under the bush after Laurette cross the road into the gap? In my mind that somebody had to be tracking her and, whoever it was, had to be the culprit that kill her.

"Why you keep asking me the same thing over and over, you is a lawyer or what? You trying to catch my tongue?"

"I'm not a lawyer. Nobody, absolutely nobody, including my mother ever tell me anything that make sense like what you telling me. I learning more from you than I learn at home."

"Agnes never put you to sit down and tell you what happen?"

"No, my mother does not bring up any conversation about Laurette."

"Pòdjab! Time and me not friends, when I see a clock, I go crazy."

"But time is important to me. It can point me to the murderer. There is not a lot of people to pick from."

"School did start already when Lovence pass. I hear the bell when it ring that morning."

"School start… Papa get there after nine. Maybe he find the body and afraid to say. What you think?" I blurt out aloud. "Why would Papa come searching for Laurette at nine? How did he know she was not in school when Mama never see him to tell him? Don't you believe, Miss Claire, that Papa did find the body already by the time he reach here?"

"Woy! Little boy, too much question; you want my head to burst?"

"If is anybody getting a headache is me. I have to know exactly where Mr Lucius was when my father come here? This thing getting bigger than my poor little head can take."

"True child? What about this old one barely holding on to my shoulders?" Miss Claire was showing signs of exasperation; I had to be careful. "If you have things to do I can come back another day."

"I tell you, the man leave here to go see 'bout his cows up the road."

"You certain it was Mr Lucius, not my father, who told you Laurette was dead?"

"Your ears not good?"

"I heard you, but in such matters I got to be exact. I want to know a little more about Mr Lucius."

"I tell you he is Teacher Merle father, my last child. What more you want me to tell you? You want to know how we come to make her too? I can tell you if you want…"

"No! No! Miss Claire, I'm not going that far. All I want is to understand. I am trying to picture that morning to place everybody where they was between eight and half past nine."

"If is picture you want you should bring a cameraman." As long as she was joking I was comfortable. "All I can tell you Laurette die after she leave here, and Lucius had go up in the heights already. That's the truth as there have a God in heaven."

"You see Mr Lucius go up the road?"

"What I watching the man for? I have food to cook and my sewing to finish, that not enough work? When Lovence come, I sure Lucius had reach the top of the road already even if he don' walk fast. He got stops to make, plenty people have to see him. He does stop an' talk with his friends to let them know where he is, in case something happen to him under the bush. That is Lucius. The morning they don' hear him coming back down the road they reaching here to check."

"There's plenty fer-de-lance in the heights, I can't blame him."

"We have a little joke between us." Miss Claire cool down again. "It does make me laugh each time I hear it. Lucius say all the snake on his land must sign his name and make race to come tell him morning once he reach, or else they can't stay there."

Thirsty for more and Miss Claire willing to talk, I did my best to steer a middle road. There would be lots of information for me to enter when I get home. "Let me see if I understand this well. School start at nine. Papa appear, then Mr Lucius. Time is key; I need time to support facts. I have to know when each one came and who was there first, where they go and who see them."

"If I didn't know you, I would say you trying to turn and twist me around. I never go to court in my life, but people say that is how lawyers behave."

"If Papa know Laurette was dead, why he didn't tell you or notify the school?" I try putting flesh on the facts as I see them: it had to be about at least an hour after Papa pass that Mr Lucius appear with the news. If Papa did not know she was dead but knew she was missing, why not go to the school and get help? The children and the teachers would be happy to go on a search.

With my imagination properly primed, I see each man as they appear on Miss Claire's doorstep. I think I know Mr Lucius and give him a face. I hear he couldn't walk fast. Papa on the other hand move like a Jeep. Miss Claire jolt me out of my thoughts. "Lovence leave here an' go back down the gap to his house. He didn't go up the road right away. I was on my machine fixing a dress for the neighbour; I didn't see when he come back by the road but I see when he pass back in hurry from the school."

"So after he come here to ask about Laurette, he go back home? Mama never say so. This is a surprise. It give Papa time to go and look for Laurette under the bush."

"Yes!" I could hardly hear Miss Claire answer.

"But Papa come back and go straight to the school. He didn't stop to tell you anything?"

"Yes, true, he didn't stop."

"I will not ask you about time, I don't want you to get vex again, but I need to know where Mr Lucius was after Papa leave the school?"

"Where he suppose to be?" Miss Claire was a bit flustered, belligerent under pressure, but I need to be clear.

"Please," I beg her. "Tell me again, between Mr Lucius and Papa, who pass first that morning?"

"Lovence pass before Lucius come back."

"Now I'm clear, I get the picture." I was feeling thirsty but dare not ask Miss Claire to stop to get me a drink of water.

Despite the pressure Miss Claire claim I was giving her, she wanted to go on: "Look, the schoolhouse still the same place, next to the church. I couldn't see who Lovence go to at the school although I can look inside the schoolyard if I want. My mind wasn't on nothing. I say he go an' see for himself if his child in school. He did have problems with two vagabonds living in the back behind the church, not far from the schoolyard. They make it a habit going in and out of jail for teefing. The bush got so much branches, didn't look strange if Lovence don' meet Laurette on the road. If you don' remember where you going an' take a wrong turn, you can get lost. I did want to ask Lovence if is Agnes that send him, it cross my mind, but..."

"I find it strange Papa didn't come back to tell you he find Laurette."

"Is Lucius that tell me… Something got to be happening, you asking so many questions one after the other; they going to call the case at last, eh?"

"I don't know; things are not too clear. Who kill my sister is all I want to find out!"

"Not just kill, your mother don' tell you?"

"Mama? All I hear from her is about Papa and how he innocent. My little brother, Marvin, don't remember Laurette and can't understand what gets into Mama when he start asking about her and Papa. He tell me so."

"If it was kill alone, you never hear how police find her? It was in the newspapers."

"Not Papa who found her? He said was him."

"Yes, he say so. He tell everybody was him, but take that with a grain of salt. When the police get there…"

"I have seen the crime scene pictures." I jump in to stop her from going into her usual long descriptions. "I notice the condition of the body, I'm not a little boy still, Miss Claire, I can face the facts."

"Naked like when she born, all her little self out; that's what I hear." Miss Claire gesticulated with both hands. "He scratch her skin just to tear off her clothes..."

"I thought you had not seen the body," I interrupt.

"People like Miss Philomene was right there with police. She come to tell me what she hear from them. The man was in a hurry to do his business; he didn't know he done kill her and was still trying to pour Gramoxone down her throat. He couldn't even take time off to fix her clothes back after he finish. That man worse than a pig."

"Why you say is a man?"

"It can't be a woman. Never! Not after what they find!"

"Then you know more than you make me think you know."

"Ah mista! There got certain things a woman does know without anybody tell her. We don' have to see anything and still we know. Not the way they find the child, legs open, breast out... The little black plastic bag with the uniform I hem still fold inside it, fling under the bush. Her clothes peel off her skin, piece by piece. Which woman doing that? They catch her by surprise as she start to climb the little hill by her house and they drag her by the leg. It got to be a strong man that do that."

In my mind I see a man dragging Laurette down the little hill by her legs to the river, and although I try hard I can't see his face. "She fight like hell all the detectives say so. She screamed, how come nobody heard?"

Miss Claire take time to answer, like she saw I was seeing something: "You think is all times you finding people under the bush. I sure your mother was at her house with your little brother and Miss Philomene was at her place. This happen right between the two houses an' nobody hear a branch break."

"In the pictures, she didn't have on much clothes but she was not naked — evidence did show she was raped."

"I tell you like I hear it. I have my reasons why I didn't want go and see her myself, she was too fresh on my mind. I would bawl down the place as if she was my child. I had bad dreams every night until the day they bury her. Everybody went to see when they bring her by the road, even schoolchildren, all the girls from her class. I hear they say she was in the sun all morning. Lovence bring a sheet from his house to cover her after the detectives take all kinds of pictures of the child. Miss Philomene was in the middle of everything. She come here straight after the hearse leave, I didn't have to ask her anything."

Miss Claire point to the spot from behind her closed shutters where the hearse was parked on the high road, near the entrance to the gap going to my parents' house. I wanted to ask about Mama and what she remembered but I dismissed the thought; it was time to leave.

When I get back to CID, Sarge gave me some tips on how he believed the sequence of events went and ask me to read through certain statements in the case file, which he insisted, corroborated his deductions. Miss Claire was not lying. What was not certain however, was whether Miss Philomene brought her up to speed, or was it bits and pieces from several people who stop by her house including Mr Lucius help her piece things together like a quilt. To me, she was close to the truth, like I imagine it. After making three daughters for three different fathers and each one following in her footsteps with their own children, some of whose children were also having children of their own, making her a great-grandmother, goes to show how far down the road her mind had travelled.

I had tried getting her to remember things eleven years before and she respond clearly. She remind me that Papa had two men arrested for touching Laurette's breasts. The incident, she said, happened in the gap to home exactly two months to the day before Laurette was killed. "The police charge the men, but the case never call. Laurette had time to die."

Miss Claire knew their names and where they live. People at Bwa Nèf got eyes and ears everywhere. They get to know things that never reach the police. I have this feeling that if I work out timelines for everybody that was in contact with Laurette that morning, one of them will stand out. Call me crazy but I remember this lesson at training school where a detective solved a case by walking a suspect to the scene of the crime using the time of death to prove he was on the spot when it happened. Might be a waste of time in this case but I must try.

# Chapter
## 4

It was early afternoon when I finally reach by my mother. It never occurred to me before how far away from the main road she live until I start coming back to visit her. Perspiration was running down my pants after I climb the little hill by our house — as a child it resembled a mountain and can still stretch my calves. The old house on pillars next to the standpipe where all of us bathed on mornings before school was a welcome sight after the long trek. I was certain Marvin, now at Dennery Secondary School, still bathed in the old concrete bath greying with mould.

Mama was always glad to see me when she came to town, but of late I notice she had a frown fixed to her face; it got worse after I start asking questions. She could not understand why I wanted to find out more about this case. She was not forthcoming, everything for her was parabol as if I was still underage and would not understand. I hate it when she take me for a child and mess with my thoughts. Since I was a policeman, it was as if I were one of those keeping her husband in jail. She had a saying: "police take an oath to arrest their own mother" so if she find herself on the other side of the law she didn't want to give me cause to put hands on her.

Before I start to ask her questions, she jump ahead: "Don't let them full you up with lies an' turn your head against your father; that's what they want. The police don' like him. They telling all his friends is he kill Laurette. Nobody does come here to see me again, except my neighbour an' she coming for a reason. From

44

the day they arrest Lovence, I tell the police they have the wrong man. But they don' listen to me. What happen there to Laurette is not Lovence do that, it not like him, he don' have a bad heart."

"If not him, who Mama? After all these years there must be something you find out, something you hear?"

"Leave me alone!" Her face in curlers ready for a fight, she never could look at me in the eye; it was like she didn't want to hear anything about Papa and the case. Maybe she was afraid I would turn her mind against her husband.

Then Mama change the subject. "Say one, say two, you never ask why Pinky always here?" Pinky was our neighbour's daughter.

"Is this something new, Mama? Something you suspect?"

"New, that's how you call it! Fafan not her son? Not he that leave an' go to the States on holiday and don' comeback?" Fafan? I remember the name; he was one of the boys that carry Laurette's coffin. "What are you saying, Mama, talk for me to understand."

"That not the same boy that say he meet Laurette in the gap coming back home from by Miss Claire?"

"You have this on your mind all this time and only now telling me?"

"Pinky here every day for news to write an' tell him about. Not from my mouth she getting it. Why he don' come down to see his grandmother that raise him. She in the house on her last legs calling his name every time the sickness give a break."

"Don't say things you can't prove, Mama."

"Can't prove? Why he didn't wait for the case to call? Because he know his name would mention. The first holiday he get after he start to work in town, he ups and go to the States and never show his face up here again.

"Mama, what you saying there is not evidence. In court the judge will shut you up, it's not even hearsay."

"And they hold Lovence on what they hear an' what people say? Leave me alone, go back where you come from. I can't change your mind; you can't change mine. You will never get me to say things to hang your father." Mama went back in her shell like a soldier crab refusing come out again until I leave.

At first, I dismiss allegations about Fafan, chalk it down to Mama's denial, frustration, anger, rage. Mama probably had a tiff with Miss Pinky, who was not the easiest of neighbours. Miss Pinky was nosey, always begging for something or the other. Nevertheless, I file the bits and pieces in my head to return to them as the evidence leads.


After many, many visits and Mama get back accustom to me around the house again, there was a day her tongue slip. She was in the kitchen in a talkative mood; I was sitting by the table watching her scale some pot fish I bring. We cover several subjects including how grateful she was for the little help I was giving her, about Marvin and his friends, her neighbours. We speak about almost everything except Papa or Laurette. Then, she start humming one of her favourite church hymns — "We stand for God and for his glory" without lifting her head from the basin and the fish. I wait until she ran out of high notes: "What you find in that hymn? You humming it non-stop since I was a little boy," I ask, pretending to joke.

She did not look at me but answered with a question: "Why you keep troubling me with all those things, eh?"

"I does find myself humming it too when I'm in trouble..." I look at her as she pick up a small fish and plunge her sharp kitchen knife into the guts. A little blood splatter on her cheeks and she wipe it away with her elbow in a rage.

"Why you don' go ask Rupert and Curtis? Your father report them for trying to rape Laurette, you forget?"

Those same two names again. Miss Claire mentioned them to me. In Mama's head, trying was doing. "Rape, Mama? I never hear they try to rape Laurette. I thought was indecent assault. If it was rape, that's serious, all like now they should be in jail." I take time off to learn more about Rupert and Curtis: their names were on police files, but not for rape or attempted rape.

"You don' live here, how you expect to know what happening up here." Mama was leading to something, perhaps she was unburdening her mind.

"I can't know if you don't tell me. What I understand is they try to touch Laurette's breasts one afternoon after school. I never hear about this rape business."

"If they try to touch her, what is that? She not their friend, she don' know them, what they want to touch her for?"

"Mama, indecent assault is not rape. I understand attempt depending on how far they go. But they never try to rip her clothes off, which means they never touch her. Papa was the one who make a big fuss, but he had no case."

"That's how it start. When it get worse Lovence go to the station and police take them down."

"Something not sounding right. Why police come all the way up here to arrest them on an indecent assault charge then let them go? What was it all about?"

"You will have to ask the police about that one."

"You telling me Rupert and Curtis know more about Laurette's death than the police?"

"You can't fool me, Andy. I is your mother I make you. Don' try an' make me think you don' know. The people you talking to only giving you half the story. They want Lovence to die in jail; one of these days they will find out when I put my two knees down an' pray for them. I know is those two maji nwè that rape my child an' that is if not them that kill her, nobody have to come and tell me."

"I don't know where to start with you. Not too long ago it was Fafan, now is Rupert and Curtis."

"Him too. All like him in it…"

"Where to begin, what to believe, God, I don't know!"

"After police arrest Lovence, I take a walk to the gadè in Belle Vue. She cut her cards an' put me straight. She see two set of hands on Laurette. Two men. She could not see their face. The doctor that look at Laurette tell Lovence the same thing. Who know these things better than a doctor…?"

"No doctor say so. We would know. It would be in his report."

"Police hold them for three months before they let them go."

"Hold them for what, Mama, rape or murder? Which of the two? That's separate charges."

"Everything. They hold them for everything but is Lovence they want. His fence low, is he they want to hang."

"Mama, you not making sense, mixing up facts, I have the reports and I can read."

"I know! All of you think I crazy, I mad. They take my husband from me, put him in jail an' you want me to still have good head? Child move in front me before I do something with you, you hear." She drop the knife in the basin with the fish and run out the kitchen.

While waiting by the high road for transport to take me to Dennery, I see an old man carrying a sack of something over his shoulder. I suppose it was ground provisions. He had a cutlass in one hand and steadied the bag with the other as he jump over the drain to go in by Miss Claire. I did not recognise him, the brim of his old felt fedora shaded his eyes, but my mind tell me it was Mr Lucius. If I can get an interview with him that would be great. I decided to try my luck. The bus to Dennery can wait.

I hurry across the high road to catch up with him. "Good afternoon, Mr Lucius." We meet outside Miss Claire's kitchen where he was washing his feet on the stones before going inside the house and was quite nimble for his age. Miss Claire was pouring water for him from a zinc bucket, measuring every drop.

"Bon apwé midi, misyé!" He answered in fine Kwéyòl, making the words flow like French embroidery.

"That's Lovence and Agnes boy. The big one that's a police," Miss Claire jump in before I could utter a word. I was not surprised when she told Mr Lucius I was a policeman. Maybe she found out after I talk to her.

"What he want?" Mr Lucius eye me from head to toe. "I got nothing to do with police. Hope he ain' come here to ask me questions."

"I just want to have a word with you." I try not to frighten him.

"He come here already; I forget to tell you. Like something happening at last with the case." Miss Claire try to whisper but I hear every word she said. "If that is so, I happy for Agnes; the longest rope got its end."

"Not around my neck!" Mr Lucius sounded sarcastic. "If you say he speak to you already, he speak to me too. If is about his father, I tell the police everything and have noffing more to say." I could not recall seeing anything from anybody name Lucius in the case files, but I knew it must be there even if under another name. In the country most times you don't know people by the names they carry on their birth certificates.

Mr Lucius signal Miss Claire to stop pouring water and climb the broken-down steps into the kitchen. He stand on the doormat wiping his feet and looking down at me. "You hear what I say?"

"I only want to ask you one thing," I said. I try to copy a page from Sarge in court when he doing cross examination: firm but not loud.

"Well ask me and finish? I can't tell you to go, is not my house." Mr Lucius was fuming.

I feel small. "You remember what time it was when you meet my father on the high road at Tèt Chimen, the day he tell you he find Laurette dead under the bush? It's important."

"You is a lawyer? You got a warrant?"

"No, sir, but..."

"Why fo you asking me questions? You not a lawyer, I not in court with you."

"I ask him that same thing too." Miss Claire turned her head away as if talking to somebody inside we couldn't see. "He never answer me straight. I tell you Lucius, something happening at last."

"I only trying to find out things for myself; I not here on police business. Up to now I know nothing about my father's case except what I read." I pretend to be frustrated. Mr Lucius could see annoyance write all over my face but he was not ready to talk.

"Ask police to tell you what I tell them. They know everything, I got no secrets; it have more than ten years since that man bring a blight on this place an' you still there asking questions. How come after all these years is me you want to tell you what happen, I not getting old? Give me a chance to forget too. Give me the little time I remain to talk to God, to see if I can make wanjman to pass through a back door when my time come. If you want to ask questions, ask the people at Bwa Nèf. Ask the detectives why they lock up Lovence before they finish their job? Why they keep him in jail so long before the case call? They bound to have a reason, your mind don' tell you something not looking right? Even a blind fool like me can see that."

My head get light, all the blood drain down to my foot. I was wasting precious time on Mr Lucius. I turn to go back to the bus stop. Walking down the track I hear my name. "Andrew, or what your name is, come here!" I freeze.

Mr Lucius remembers my name but pretend to forget everything else. I see Miss Claire whispering in his ears. "You is a full policeman now?" Mr Lucius talk like my sergeant, a lot of power in his voice.

He make me a sign, come; I follow him inside to the kitchen table. "You eat anything yet for today?" Miss Claire ask and I lie. Mr Lucius invite me to sit with him. "Since you eat already, you can fire one with me?" He smile through his gums. Miss Claire dig up a demijohn half full of mix from under the table and pull two clean glasses out from an ancient cabinet. The brown mahogany stain evaporate leaving the smooth grain exposed. She did not sit with us and went to the stove to warm Mr Lucius' dinner. The two of us were alone, but you could feel Miss Claire's two ears sticking out like a TV antenna, listening.

Every vehicle I hear going down the road send me to the edge of my chair. I did not want to miss the transport back to Dennery town or else I would have to spend the night by my mother, which I did not relish. "You don' have to worry," Mr Lucius said, "I can smell the vans from Tèt Chimen coming a mile away." He poured himself a stiff drink.

"You doing that so long it must be a habit by now." I try to keep the conversation alive.

After the first shot went down his throat, his tongue get loose; he squeeze his eyelids, making his eyes look smaller — could have been the rum prancing in his stomach. "You don' think police make a mistake?" I was speechless. Expect the unexpected, first lesson in true detective work, yet I was unprepared.

"You was only a kwichet when police take Lovence down. I feel sorry for you and your little brother — what his name is again?" He was giving me the absentminded shuffle but I was not falling for it, I knew better.

"My father or my brother?" I asked him.

"I know Lovence. Your brother name I forget."

"Marvin, you can only catch him on weekends."

"I can see you don' know nothing. I hope you strong to take what you find. Long time people use to say, don' trouble the dead unless the dead trouble you. You know what I talking about, eh?"

"Yes!" I pretend to know. "You hit the nail on the head fast."

"People always know more than police. You know that's true or else you wouldn't come all the way up here to talk to me." I smile, he wasn't waiting for answers. "I don' have endikasyon, but I not stupid. You got to look out for your family whether it's good blood or bad blood, that law there from the time God make the world. After we get to know where we come from, we can choose, but we can't run away an' hide from what we born to be."

That was deep. Mr Lucius lose me with his thoughts, but I could tell him, I understand. People where I work say things to hurt me, they are those that don't like me, but I learn to remain cool and take it as it come.

"A lot of things does be true once you can see the smoke — but?" Mr Lucius stress on the 'but'. "Most times what you hear is lies. You ask me when your father tell me about your sister. To speak the truth, I didn't have that on my mind when I meet him.

I don' carry wristwatch, I tell time by the sun, once it don' rain I alright. What I can tell you, when I meet him at Tèt Chimen, I did finish tie my cow, an' leave Gwan Bwa coming back. I cut a small bunch of bannann the wind throw down during the night an' was carrying it on my shoulder. I didn't stay long in the pasture that morning; it was as if I know something was going to happen. I did hear things, people talking; some a dem say from the time the child start having breasts the man did want her for wife and Agnes was not doing nothing to stop him. Anyhow, that's not what you here to talk about."

Something in me snap, I had to check myself to make sure I was hearing right, although I am not sure he took notice.

Before I could stop him he was off again. "I see Lovence up Tèt Chimen, by the lay-by where we waiting to take transport. He look like somebody that going mad. His hair didn't know what we call comb, his clothes chifonnen hungry for iron. I tell myself, Agnes ain' see when he leave the house, but I can't tell him nothing, he's a big man. No way she would let him go by the road like that.

"Lovence see me and come on the other side to talk, his mouth could hardly open. He say, 'I meet my child dead under the bush by the house.' He say it just like I telling you now, plain, simple, no fuss. I didn't know what he talking about; it take a while to understand, you don' hear these things every day. It hit me hard in my stomach; a fwison take me in all my bones like I pass on a wire with electric an' it run straight to my head. I couldn't lift my tongue to speak. When I catch myself, all I could ask him, is where he goin. He tell me he reaching by his aunty, Miss Eldra, but he done pass the house. I ask him, if he call the police already, he tell me no. I shake my head, you have to drop everything and call the police or else, your right going to turn your wrong.

"He say he got so much on his mind he don' know where to start. We walk back together down the road 'til we reach Miss Eldra house. I beg him again, before you do anything, call the police. I stop an' watch him go inside the house, I did want to follow him, a little voice tell me keep my tail between my legs. I pick up speed an' come down the road fast-fast with load on my shoulder, my belly boiling, the hard pitch lighting a fire under my foot; you'd think I do something and police behind me. When I reach here, I couldn't hold it again; I throw the sack and the bunch of bannann down on the kitchen floor with my cutlass and run straight to the latrine before I could say anything to anybody. I even forget to take paper."

Whether details matched what Mr Lucius say to detectives years ago I didn't have a clue, I still had to find his statement. However, I did not want to stop him. I was interested in something he start telling me about earlier concerning Papa going behind Laurette. He claim he hear about it from the people in the village. How did they know? I live in the house and never see anything to make me suspicious. Even if I was underage, I would suspect.

Mr Lucius grin. "You must always listen to the people that is God voice speaking."

"You can't hold a man on what you hear people say."

"But the police still hold him, although I can't say for sure is he do it. I didn't see, but people saying is he, nobody else. I hear the child did swear to God she was going to report him to the police the last time he go behind her and that is why he run quick and put the blame on the two bolomns living behind the church."

"Rupert and Curtis?"

"You see I not lying, you know their name."

"Mr Lucius! Suspicion by itself is not evidence."

Notwithstanding everything he said, there was no evidence, only hearsay. Good gossip to steer me in the right direction. I write everything down as best as I can remember without adding my grain of salt to the soup. What Mr Lucius had to say help me to corroborate some things Miss Claire said but very little else. Was my father an innocent victim of incompetent investigators and was being held while they searched for real evidence? All those years are more than enough to get to the truth or let the man go.

# Chapter
## 5

On my agenda. I plan a visit to Rupert and Curtis but delayed it a bit wanting to learn more about the two. They were veterans, with rap sheets longer than the years on their head: praedial larceny, burglary and theft, purse snatching, obscene language and other petty crimes, nothing major. What I read in the evidence file was sketchy. I needed more meat on the bone or else they would bamboozle me with jailhouse tactics, which, Sarge tell me, they were quite good at. I keep him abreast of my plans. He said there was nothing wrong if I choose to interview the two men again. Once I did not make them think I was doing these interviews to provoke them was OK with him. "I don't like them anyway," he told me. "I would be happy if you could find something to keep them inside for good."

Back at work, I went straight to Papa's case file and search for statements by Rupert and Curtis. I compare what I find with what Mr Lucius said and other people that meet Papa that morning. "You don't think I should interview my father before I speak to them?"

"No!" Sarge shouted. You could hear him a block away. "The DPP bring charges against your father already. I want no interference. I can't stop you from going to see your father, but please, don't talk about the case if you go."

"I not stupid. I never went to see the man; only my mother goes. I will always tell you first."

"You had better. For your own sake. Keep far way."

"If I go what you think he going to tell me?"

"Detective! An open mind…"

"I have my suspicions. While I can't accuse or acquit, I smell a heap of rotten fish floating on that sea."

"Good," Sarge said. "Once you know your place, there is no conflict with the defence. Remember your father is out of bounds to you in this investigation. Sometimes you got to follow your nose, but your nose can be wrong, especially when you too close to the smell."

"So you saying I must not see him like a son either?"

"No, I'm not saying so. All I asking is be careful."

"I confess, with all that's not happening, sometimes I feel like going and see him."

"You can feel but take your time; you need a clear head."

In accepting Sarge's advice I limit my pace although I did not think he was right. What my father had to say was important to me. But! That's a big one for me and my conscience. There were lots of people I wanted to talk to, but they were not ready to talk to me yet. They were waiting for the case to call and for the court to rule before they speak.

On my next weekend off I decide to go to the country and spend some time with my mother. My girlfriend, Angel, was not happy that I was going alone, and at the last minute I agree to take her with me. Her belly was big and showing already. We reach a little before dark and went straight to my mother's house. Mama fall in love with Angel on the spot and allow her to sleep with her on the bed. I stay on the floor with Marvin, who wasn't little anymore. His body was spreading out like any teenager, hinting at muscles and his voice cracking when he speak, somewhere between man and boy.

My ears had forgotten the night sounds that come in to the

house from under the bush when darkness come. There was clack-clack in the tall trees, fer-de-lance and tète chien arguing under the bush about who own what side of the ravine, while the wind whistle through tall bamboo on either side of the riverbank like when male cats lose their wives and go searching for them. I had forgotten co-ke-o-ko fore-day morning in the coconut trees, until I hear it again with the fowl cocks in the Julie mango tree behind the kitchen. Once in a while, a dog would howl in the distance when a machine race up the high road, or a cat scream after a rat make it jump. Mama always keep a cat in the kitchen to prevent mice from interfering with her food. In our part of the country there's always something to wake you up during the night but sleep would take you in the end. Before I could bat my eyes however, the fowl cocks had gone hoarse and daylight reach straining its eyes through holes in the boards. Morning come with church bells, and before I know it, it was dawn.

Angel was still asleep when I get up to go outside to pass water in my mouth — I forgot my toothbrush back in Castries and borrowed hers. Mama was already in the kitchen. I stand in the open, my back to the house, like when I was small and peed down the little hill before I passed a wash rag with some soap on my face.

"You not forgetting your bad manners, eh Andy?" I hear Mama's voice; it come from inside the kitchen. She was in good spirits. After I scrub my teeth, I went to the kitchen, sit in the old chair that's been around from before I was born. Mama hand me a cup of coffee, hot like she know I like it, black and very sweet.

"I see Angel almost ready," Mama said, trying to make small talk.

"She still has some months to go." I blushed.

"You all have a name for the baby yet?"

"If is a girl, we will call her Laurette. We don't think it will be a boy."

"If is a boy call him Lovence." I couldn't believe she was serious.

"We'll see about that when the time comes." I force myself to smile, but a smile just couldn't come to my face.

Mama was ready to jump all over me to defend her husband. "Lovence didn't do nothing wrong, you of all people know that." Something in her voice told me she was not herself. "You think he would touch a child he bring up an' feed from a baby?"

"Why is he still in jail then, Mama?" I was uncertain how this would sound in her ears.

"I don' know." She started to cry hiding her face as usual in a dark corner.

"Mama, how many times I will say it, I'm not little again. There's no need to hide things from me."

"I not hiding things from you!" She could have blown my head off with a gun if she had one and would be none the wiser in my coffin. That's how angry she got all of a sudden.

"I hearing things every day that make me afraid. I don' go by the road again unless I have to go."

"Mama, stop listening to people, they will send you mad."

"Which people? Sometimes just I can't take it; it's too much!"

"Tell me what you hear, Mama. What making you feel afraid? Tell me." I watch tears roll down her cheeks faster than the little ravine we call river below the house.

Mama wipe her eyes with her skirt and stare at me. Her lips move spitting out words. "Your father is not Laurette father." It had been like a cancer inside her; it took a lot to spit it out.

"I know," I said.

"How you know? I never tell you…" Suddenly, I see fear in her eyes; a child about to get licks.

"I am a detective. My job is to find out things."

"The police know too and is for that they holding Lovence."

"That's not a crime. You meet your madam when she already got one child; you love her, so you take the child and raise it like it's yours. That's life."

"Nobody tell me, but I know. Is because Lovence not Laurette father they putting everything on his back."

"I don't agree, and you know well it's not so, Mama. You know a lot more than me; you never leave this house. Everything that happen here under this roof, you see, you hear, you know."

"Why everybody saying so? I don' know nothing." A fresh crop of tears appear.

"You must see certain signs like Laurette's clothes getting too small, men looking hard at her even when she's with you. You hear stories from school about boys looking under her dress. Don't tell me you so blind not to notice what's happening right under your nose."

"Eh ben, Andy, put it on my back. Why is me?"

"His lawyers know. Whether I believe them or not is another matter."

"The lawyers don' speak to me. They tell Lovence they don' want me to talk to people about the case, the judge will think is konplo. When I ask the lawyers questions, I get more confuse so I not asking them before they say I troublesome an' leave Lovence to finish the rest of his life in jail."

"Listen to yourself? You hear what you just said? Stop talking like one of those ignorant people that didn't go to school, Mama."

"I didn't go to high school like you. I leave in standard…" Before she start rehearsing her life story I cut her short; I hear it so many times and know it by heart; it's her main line of defence to back out of corners. "Police can't hold Papa forever unless a jury find him guilty."

"They have him and they not letting him go."

"That's not true, Mama!"

"Who else they ever hold for so long without bail?"

"Quite a few. You can't blame the police for that. The fault is the court."

"If they can't bring a case what they keeping him inside for?"

"You would be surprised." I rattle through my mind to find something she might not have heard about. "You know Papa renew his passport the week after Laurette die? Detectives find that out from immigration after they arrest him." I been dying to tell her from the day I heard but didn't have the guts.

"What you mean?"

"It look like he was planning to leave the country."

"Leave me an' my children to go where?" Mama sighed, long and deep. "They know he innocent so they got to find all kind of excuse to keep him. Before I know Lovence he make money in the States cutting cane. If things hard over here, you don' think he will want to go back?"

"Without telling his wife and children?"

"Who say he didn't tell me?" I feel flustered with Mama on the defensive; this happens every time she's worried. If I was alone I would pack up and leave. I fake my best good-nature face not wanting to rile her more: "I know better, if you just stay quiet and listen to yourself sometimes, Mama, you will learn a lot."

Maybe what I said help calm down Mama for a short while although she start acting up again after I get up to go out in the yard for some fresh air. "You come all the way from Castries to ask me questions. How you think I feel? Well, let me go first, if is listen you want me to listen to you, why you not making them let go your father? Lovence is your father, you know, so why you not asking them the same questions you asking me? Why is me you come all this way to harass?"

"Mama, I don't know everything, I am trying hard to find answers myself and you not making it easy."

"Like is you alone in this…"

"You were there, on the spot, his wife, I was still a child. You see Laurette before the hearse take her away. You see the marks on her; her clothes peel off like yam skin from her body; it was your sheet Papa take to cover her after the doctor finish with his exam. Help me, please Mama, help me to find the truth. That's all I want from you."

Mama settle a bit while I was speaking and look calm yet refuse to tackle the subject head on. I couldn't help thinking, she was shutting out the truth.

"You can't let your father stay an' rotten in jail. If you stand up for him, you'll see what will happen. Don't do like the others an' talk against him as if he's a stranger. Don't go round in rum shop like those other police an' bad mouth him because he not there to answer for himself."

"Laurette can't answer for herself." I couldn't let her see the smirk on my face. Mama knows this kind of tactics will not work on me but it didn't make sense aggravating a bad situation. With Mama at her best, I could not win, not when she climb on her high horse. I was a policeman, and the police was holding her husband, who was also my father. In her mind I have the power to set him free and was doing nothing about it: no judge wants to grant him bail, no lawyer wants the case, but she thinks little me can change that.

I bathe under the old standpipe and put on fresh clothes. Don't know if it was the cologne I splash on my skin to remove the blue soap smell which woke up Angel. I saw her through the tiny mirror, sitting up on the bed, looking at me, her eyes wanting to ask questions.

"I going by the high road," I said before she ask, without turning around.

She didn't know the whole story about Papa, at least not from me. I didn't know how much her mother, Miss Beatrice, tell her, but it could not be more than what was in the papers. I feel ashamed and did not want to bring her into the picture frame too soon. We were not married yet, my conscience would not allow, not so soon anyway. She thought my job make me keep details secret. She never probe until matters affect me to an extent where our relationship seem in jeopardy.

Angel was a real angel by name and nature. I always say I was the luckiest man in the world the day I lose my way in the Ministry Building and ask her for directions on the elevator. She look at me sideways as if afraid, saying in her mind, what that man looking at me so for.

"You don't have to be scared," I tell her. "I'm a police officer." (Although I was still a recruit at training school.)

She look at me without smiling. "That's when I should be afraid."

"What happen, you lose your smile?" I ask putting on my best sexy tone.

The elevator reach third floor. "This is where you going," she said as the door open.

"What about you?"

"One up!"

"When I finish, can I come to see you?" The door closed without getting a reply, no chance to put in a comma edgewise.

Something strange was happening to me. I could not control myself from wanting to see her again. Attractive — a little plain face, no lipstick, no earrings. She look new to the job like me, fresh from school. I wondered if she had a boyfriend or was having a crush on somebody. Two weeks after our first encounter, on my way to the ATM to get some weekend money, who should I see going in the same direction?

"Hello!" I shout jockeying to get abreast. She did not answer. I skip forward faster and catch up with her.

"Not you again!" She glared. "You tracking me or what?"

"Oh no! I will never do that."

"You men! I don't know what to believe when you speak."

"You sound defensive." I brave the choppy waters.

"I not afraid of you." She look at me under her eyelids like somebody wearing glasses; her eyes were brown. "What's your name?" she asked.

Too stun to speak, I pause before opening my mouth. "Andrew, friends call me Andy."

"I don't know why I talking to you. My mother warn me about policemen."

"I not a full policeman yet."

"I hear you!" She nipped and increase her speed.

"I'd like very much to be your friend," I stutter, afraid of what she might reply.

"I don't have boyfriends."

"That means I'll be the first?"

"Maybe? If you have guts to face my mother... Thank God, she keeps all of you away."

"I'm sure your mother is a nice person." A little voice tell me I doing much better than I believe, but don't get overconfident. "If I must ask your mother to be your friend I will. You want me to ask her?"

"You are strange." She shrug her shoulders and smile at me.

"Why you say so?"

"You don't ask me my name; you don't ask for my phone number and you want to meet my mother." We laughed.

"I am Angel. I'm a receptionist on the fourth floor." She pointed at the building behind us where we met on the elevator.

"Please to meet you Angel."

We shake hands and exchange phone numbers; I walk her back to the building after she complete her transactions, pressed the button to the fourth floor and watch her disappear. I was so happy meeting Angel; I forget what I come to do. I hurry back to the bank only to find a queue waiting at the machine.

It was easy to keep Angel out of my mind during the day with so many things to do at training school: shoeshine, weaponry, the drills and everything else in between. However, nighttime she comes barging in and I can't stop her. I pick up a habit of passing by her office every time I go to that part of town and look up hoping to see her in one of the windows, until I find the nerve to take the elevator to the fourth floor. As soon as I come through the revolving door, there she was at the counter: "Can I help you, officer?" Her voice chiming like a clock.

"Just pass to say hello. Haven't seen you by the ATM lately."

"I don't live there," she was quick to reply.

There's something about this girl, like a magnet drawing me in, I could not hold back.

"I wanted to call, but didn't want you to think I'm fresh." I prayed hard for her to grin.

"How you know I don't believe you're fresh?"

"You'll always give me the benefit of the doubt."

She blushed. "I did wonder, how come he hasn't called, but maybe you been too busy with the chicks."

"No, not that, shy maybe." I moved away from the counter back towards the door. I noticed she smiled and every pore in me open.

"Thanks anyway for the speed visit." I disappeared on a cloud and float all the way down to ground level.

That evening, elated, bold enough to break through the ice, I wait until a little before the seven o'clock news on TV to call. Her phone ring until it rang off. I concoct a series of scenarios in my mind. Maybe she turns her phone off at home, her mother must be strict, no calls while at home or she is out with friends; maybe, maybe, maybe?

My cell rang at quarter to nine. It was Angel. "Hello!" I whisper. "Thanks for calling back."

"Surprise, surprise! At last!"

"What you mean? I promise to call and I did."

"So I see!"

"I thought of you alone at home flicking through the TV channels."

"I am never alone and I have more important things to do than watch television."

"Then I can visit you in between, sometimes, may be take you out on weekends."

"You moving fast, Mister Andy! I have to clear things with my mother first."

"That's OK. Let me know as soon as she gives clearance."

Angel laughed. "Now you take me for a joke."

"No, I am dead serious. Look at my face!"

"Where, through the phone? Poor you, sensitive man! I will let you know."

"Can I call you again tomorrow?"

"What's the hurry? You have a chick there with you? Sorry to disturb!"

"Don't hang up! There's nobody here; I am alone."

"Just testing."

"Can I call, no objections?

"I gave you my number, didn't I?" I wait for the click at her end before hanging up.

Having slept well, next day I never felt the heat on the parade grounds. I had a dislike for morning parades — the sun always shine hot on our backs. That morning, I didn't feel it thinking about Angel and dreaming about the all-clear to visit her. I call her at work that afternoon a little before four thirty. She said she was in the Ladies powdering her face. I was tempted to ask if she was dolling up for me, but no. "Last night I couldn't talk," she said. "My mother was there listening. Don't think she didn't ask about you; she wants to know which man I give my number."

"What did you say?"

"I told her but left out the policeman part."

"What?"

"If you know what I say, I tell her I find you strange."

"What she said?"

"Nothing!"

"Nothing? That's good or bad?"

"I tell her you want to meet her."

"Whaaat?"

"You really strange in truth."

"That's all?"

"What else you want? You want her to like you — she doesn't know who you are."

I still get flashbacks: Angel and I, two strangers walking in the same direction, the same road, each careful where to place our foot until we could level with one another. Suddenly, we mould into a single cell understanding one another's pain without having to talk about it. There was no better understanding between us than thinking about Angel and hearing the phone ring.

# Chapter
## 6

Mama smile when she realise she was getting another hand in the kitchen at least for the Sunday meal and that revive her spirits. Her conversation change. She couldn't stop making remarks about what a nice daughter-in-law I give her. She went on and on up until I was ready to head out of the house. I left and went down the track to the high road to pay Rupert and Curtis a visit. I cross the high road, rush pass Miss Claire's house without shouting out good morning — I didn't want to be seen, or else the news would be all over Bwa Nèf before my shirt tail disappeared around the cemetery wall.

I hear singing; it came from the church. I pick the best time for my mission when everybody at mass. The cemetery wall was high enough to hide me — built in stone with lime around most of the graveyard, except for the front, which had a barbed wire fence and a wooden gate to keep out sheep and goats and sometimes two-leg strays. Once around the wall, you could not be seen from the road or the church. Not too many people chose to live behind the cemetery. They were very superstitious at Bwa Nèf — digging around graves for old bones to use in their black magic ceremonies. Don't mind all the radios blaring when you travel up the road and TV antennae like flagpoles sticking out of every other kitchen roof. Just mention you see a shadow hanging around the cemetery with a piece of rope round its neck or a man riding a three-leg donkey on full a moon night up Gwan Bwa, right away you have a panic on your hands. In this little place where everybody believe in God, they have equal faith in the devil.

As I approach the old kitchen standing on one leg by itself in the corner of somebody's yard, canting over like it about to fall in the drain on the side, I feel a heat pass behind my head and muscles in my hands and legs contract. That does happen only when I ready for action. Feet heavy, like they weigh down with stones, but not from fear. These guys are two criminals, why should I bother if I show them my rough side? There was a new wall house nearby, which make the old kitchen look even more obvious standing alone in a clean yard that sweep daily. Somebody was trying hard to keep the old kitchen alive, patching it with pieces of cardboard and old tin cans. A window, hinges creaking, swings with the breeze on the side over the drain. A couple of barrel covers still showing their distillery marks nail to the side facing the cemetery to keep out spirits, I presume, laughing at my own little joke.

Close up, the kitchen look like it was at one time an oven, the only entrance was a two-piece door half open, facing the morning sun. I peep in. Inside is black with soot, too dark to see anything, but if anybody is in there I hope I would see them before they get the upper-hand on me. I shout a loud good morning, nobody answer. I repeat, good morning again, in my policeman voice this time and two people jump like jumbie out from the dark.

"Morning!" They answer together. "I looking for Rupert and Curtis," stern as I can be. "You know where I can find them?" I try to find their eyes, but they turn their heads away from the light that was coming through directly behind me. It seem I wake them up; they smell like two ram goats let out in a pasture to find a mate. One of them ask, "Who is you?" He spoke rough.

"That's not important," I said.

"Well make it important, or leave us alone," the other one, who I could not well see, barked.

"You is Andrew, Lovence son. The policeman?" The same voice again, my eyes were adjusting to the darkness inside.

"It look like you know me before I get to know you."

"We does see you when you go by your mother." I still could not see his face.

"An' by Miss Claire," the other character said.

It make no sense to remain a mystery. Better to know where you stand than having to guess was one of the things Sergeant Willius drummed into me.

"You know why I'm here?" I lean on the bottom half of the two-piece door and finger the bolt.

"No! What we do now?" The one who was more brazen reply. "You only have to go to jail once an' dem fellas mark you for life."

"I am here about an old story." I try to compose myself. "Laurette, my sister." I hear a rustle when I mention her name like the wind going through the old kitchen. A short nervous silence took over before somebody spoke again.

"We tell de police everyting. Dey take it down, an' make us mark our name in de book." One of the characters appear from the shadows; his hair hadn't seen a comb in years.

"Which one of you is Rupert?"

"I." The one nearest to me raise his hand like we did in school when teacher ask a question.

"So you're Curtis?" I point to the other one hiding behind him. I notice a blank look on his face; mouth wide open baiting flies and showing more than a few rotten teeth. Dry spit cake around both corners of his lips, jittery, like somebody who hadn't passed water in his mouth yet for the morning and was afraid I catch a smell. I call out his name like roll call and he tap his partner on the shoulder as if asking him to explain.

"Dat's Ma Lovence son, Miss Agnes. She living in de back by where we use to cut kannèl for Miss Grainy. He's a policeman!"

"How come Miss Agnes son is police?" Curtis ask his partner. "He not Laurette brother?"

"You see what dat happening dere, eh." Rupert shook his head. The two men were bareback, still in underwear. I could see every rib sticking out of their chests. They did not seem to have had a good meal in days and the trembling I was seeing could be malnutrition.

"De police hold us and beat us every time," Curtis said. "Policeman is not our friend."

"Dey beat us non-stop wid a hot towel under our foot." Rupert supported him, repeating almost word for word.

"If dat was all dey do us," Curtis continued. "Dey take us by the beach, bar our eyes an' force us to swim in de sea." I grin. Sarge told me about our friend, the corporal's favourite techniques that helped to loosen tongues.

"I tink I was going to drown," Rupert said, pretending to be afraid.

"That's ages ago, you survived. So what's all the fuss now?"

"I don' forget people dat do me wickedness," Rupert said.

"Time to forget, man! You're alive, move on!"

"I sure you not forgetting your sister," Rupert was quick to reply.

"Sure right on that score; I wouldn't be here if I did. The man who blindfold you and send you to swim in the sea is no longer in the force. Nowadays, police can't do these things."

"He go, but he leave his tricks behind... I would a like to bounce up wid him in jail. He an' de same ones dat try to drown me because I refuse to say I strangle Laurette. I would show dem how sweet jail is." A smile broke across his face thinking of revenge and he apologised in his own style. "I don' know noffing about your sister, I can't help you. But ask your father, ask Mr Lovence, he know. Is he make police arrest us for noffing."

"Always for noffing, until we find out de truth."

"We didn't do noffing," Rupert stressed, trembling. "Your father is he to check; he know what he do. He call police an' make dem arrest us twice. First time he say is for touching Laurette in de gap, and next time, for…" He couldn't bring himself to saying the word.

"Look in your big book at de station, everyting in it," says Curtis. "He in your jail, why you don' make him talk. He make police take me and Rupert. He say Laurette tell him how we try to touch her breast and lift up her skirt. Dat day we never see de child. How he can say is we? When Laurette die, he tell police is we dat kill her. You all know well dat not true but is us you behind… Don' take me down, please, I can't go back inside again, dey doing me fings inside." Curtis was crying big tears.

"Shut up, Curtis!" Rupert get bad.

"Rupert!" I shout his name to gain attention. "Where were you the morning Laurette died? Don't tell me you forget."

"Me?" Curtis ask.

I look at him and shake my head. "Not you — Rupert! You bound to remember what you was doing."

"On a minivan goin' to Castries." Rupert was ready with his answer.

"Where you was?" Curtis asked, as if cross-examining me.

"In school."

"I was wid Rupert," he said. "I was on de bus too."

"Two of you went to Castries to do what? You work there?"

"We was goin to look for work," Rupert said.

"You got work?"

"No!" Both replied together like they practise the drill.

"What did you do in Castries?"

"We walk," Rupert said.

"You walked too, Curtis?"

"Him and me, we buy a plate of food by de market and..."

"With what money? What kind of food?"

"Bouyon!" Rupert seemed please. "It did have 'nough donbwé and peas, not enough meat."

"You have a good memory, man. All these years and you remember every little thing just like that?"

"Police always asking us de same questions." Rupert smiled. To him it was a smart thing to say.

"If we forget, we dead," Curtis added, breathing hard like he just climb a steep hill.

"Now, let's go back to the beginning, the day you touch Laurette's breast?"

"Me! Not me!" Rupert shouted. "What I touchin her breast for? Ever see me have a girlfriend?

"You hate women?"

"I don' reach that far with you, Officer," Rupert growled at me.

"Don't get me mad now! The two of you go everywhere together. Which one of you touched her?"

"Touch? I don' know about touch!" Curtis was humble.

"I don' know is not an excuse! Police arrested both of you, something happened, either both to blame, or one covering for the other."

"I was not dere," Curtis griped. "Ask Roderick, de minivan driver."

Roderick was my mother's friend. He was a bus driver and

sometimes he took me all the way to Dennery to school on Monday mornings without having me to pay for the ride. Was there a connection between Roderick and Laurette? He was older than her by far. I never heard that angle before. While Curtis is telling me to check Roderick, other thoughts are entering my policeman mind. Roderick was already a big man with his own minivan; Laurette was still in school, although without her uniform she look grownup — a full pair of breasts and large hips. Could it be? Suspicion, suspicion, no stone must be left unturned.

"He was always chattin her by de gap, bringin sweetie for her when he come from town." Rupert looked at me sideways. "Noffing for dat? No police come an' arrest him. He got a van, he's a big shot. But little me with noffing in my pocket, dat never have a woman, far less a girlfriend, is me you want to hang." Rupert's tongue was wagging; I hit a sore spot.

"Don't matter to me who you want or what you like, what I need to know right now is why my father chose the two of you to bring charges against? There must be some smoke. If none of you touch Laurette, what make him say you did? She had to tell him something; things like this don't just stay so and happen."

"Is if she tell him anyting," Curtis said.

"That we will never know. Laurette is not here to talk for herself."

"So you asking us to talk for her?" Curtis posited.

"Shut up, Curtis!" Rupert was blue vex. "Your father in the station with you. Ask him." He look at me cross-eye puffing out his chest. "Maybe he self touch her and when she say she goin' to tell her mother, he put de blame on us to save face."

I went silent to gather my thoughts, these two are good, damn good. "What make you say that?" My mind was still processing his last remarks and expecting more.

"You forget how de man use to go by de schoolhouse on afternoons and march de child home?"

"Because he hear some boy was walking with her in de gap," Curtis added his piece.

Once or twice, I recall Papa come in the schoolyard and ask the teacher for permission to take Laurette home because her mother want her. As a child that didn't mean nothing. All children had to run when parents call, but this was a new angle. I was curious: "What boy? You remember his name?"

"You beginning to listen to me, eh, dat's very good." Rupert stretched as if to remove the last traces of sleep from his muscles. "Miss Pinky son; don' know his real name, everybody call him Fafan."

Now there were two new names — Roderick and Fanfan. It was important that I remain cool and slowly digest what I was learning. Keep an open mind was what I been taught.

"He take in front an' run to police." Curtis looked sad; something was bothering him; it could be his conscience. He was not crying, his eyes look dry, but I could see water gathering in the corners.

"Nice little girl, who would want to touch her breast? Not me, I not no animal, I don' do—" He stop suddenly as if he forgot what he was about to say and start to cough.

"I wouldn't know where to start," Rupert add without a drop in pace. "A lot of boys did want her; she was good-looking, nice shape."

"How you know?"

"People talk, I hear, I listen when big man talk…"

"A lot of big man too, eh, big like you?" I was hoping to provoke them, but they smart, they remain silent; you'd think they didn't hear me. Crimes by men against women come from a desire to show power, especially if they feel they got none. I gone back to the textbook for a minute, and the glove fit Rupert and Curtis, making them perfect suspects.

Curtis spoke after a short silence. "A lot of big man like her father did want her; I see dem in de shop when she come to make message rolling dere eyes, licking dere lips like dey thirsty, feeling up dere crotch — everywhere too hot."

I could not take their words for granted; it would be ridiculous to believe those two without other validating evidence. They had been to prison and masters at redirecting suspicion. "Come on guys, don't waste my time, I not giving up!"

Curtis cringe. Rupert fold his arms and face me. "Your father use to beat your mother every day after you an' your sister go to school, noffing for dat?"

My mouth open wide. I could not hide the surprise. "You hear well!" Rupert was rubbing it in. I see these tactics use many times — shifting blame to somebody else to save your skin. Children play this trick well in the schoolyard. I quickly composed myself to ask: "How you know so much about my father and I never see you by our house?"

"When we work for Miss Grainy on her land behind your mother's house, we can hear your mother when she scream," Rupert said.

"She use to scream loud for people to hear," Curtis added his piece.

I wanted to shout, stop it, but needed to hear more. "Miss Grainy, the old lady on the hill above us?" I had no question ready but pretend to inquire knowing full well there was only one Miss Grainy near us.

"Yes," Rupert answered. "We can see everyting inside your house when we up dere."

"An' we can hear." Curtis tried to look sad.

"You can't see our house through the bush." I was adamant. I thought I know the place, I roam all about the bush as a boy, but not enough, it would seem.

"Who say?" Curtis butt in. "Once your mother door open, we seein all inside."

"How come I never see you?" I was looking for a loophole to trap him.

"We pass a next road, on de odder side, from Tèt Chimen, it puttin us right by de basen," Curtis said.

"An' up de back road, up de hill to reach Miss Grainy place. You don' know when we dere." Rupert try his best to clarify.

"What time you went by Miss Grainy the morning my father find Laurette under the bush?"

"All de time we telling you we go to Castries you not listening to us! Wha happen, you tink we lyin? " Rupert moaned. "See for yourself Curtis; when I tell you dat man tryin' to trick us, say it not true. Miss Grainy don' want us on her land when she not dere, she tell everybody we does steal her fings. She pay us for the work we do an' say she will call us when she want us again," he explained.

"Did you speak to Miss Grainy that morning?

"What morning? No!" Rupert was upset. "I tell you she was not dere."

I sense him fighting to stick to his story. "We didn't go near her land dat morning." He look at me straight to speak.

"How you know she was not there?"

"Ah Officer, don' try dat?" I anticipate any moment he could break.

"She self tell us," Curtis said, at the same time begging Rupert stay calm.

"After she pay us, she say she have to go Dennery in de morning, she not going to be dere, don' come," Rupert stammered to make his point.

"What time she tell you all that?"

"Time! Time again! You see me with wristwatch? Last time I see her was when we finish work de afternoon an' she pay us. Watch this man, Curtis, he smart."

"Anybody see you coming from under the bush that morning?" My question was directed to Rupert. His eyes blink, both hands were shaking. Curtis take in front before he could come up with an answer.

"We go under de bush to do our business, who see, see. We don' have latrine. I finish first and come down de road by Mr Paulinos. I see your sister come down de little road from by Miss Claire an' cross de street, she was running. She have a bag in her hand."

"Curtis!" I could see Rupert fuming all over. "Dat's why I don' like taking you behind me where I go."

"She was in a hurry to reach home to dress for school," I said. I needed to put some peace between the two. "You see anybody following her?"

"No." Curtis seemed sure.

"What time was it when you see Laurette, Curtis?"

"What you got wid time, like you married to it? Everyting for you is time, time, time." Rupert leap ahead.

"I don' know time." Curtis drop his voice to speak.

"We don' have clock, I tell you!" Rupert shout.

These guys were not simple. My friend, the corporal, with all his unorthodox procedures could not break them. There were a few new things I learn from them, new persons of interest for me to follow up, and the big one: the story of Papa beating Mama while Laurette and I at school. While I did not believe them, I could not shake off the image of Mama being ill-treated by the man she love so bad who also happen to be my father. Mama could have been a little afraid of him but would go toe to toe in an argument. Is true, she always walk a step behind him sticking in his heels like a pussy cat and carrying out all his requests without question. Everything from washing and ironing his clothes, bringing his food to him in the bedroom when he decide to stay in bed; fetching him a glass of water at the click of his fingers. When he scream his head off, she stop what she is doing and go all hands, eyes and ears to him. But I never saw signs of abuse. Maybe I was too young.

Another point, but this one is harder. Did Mama ever hear about the rumour around the village that Papa must have been interfering with Laurette, or did Mama think Laurette was fed up with him beating her and was to going to report him to the police? Each had its own kind of trouble. Don't know when I can get around to Mama to sit down for a long chat. I would have to stay clear of her hands; a slap could come down on me before I blink. But if some of the things I hearing is true, they point to motive; and that's the one thing I cannot find anywhere in the files.

# Chapter
## 7

Up the road I went towards Tèt Chimen hoping to find Mama's favourite driver. For years she climb aboard his transport when she want to go anywhere far, swearing he was the safest thing on the high road, never had an accident, the only one to take her from Bwa Nèf and put her down in front my nennenn house in Dennery. Roderick was on my shortlist among persons I had to interview; not as a suspect, but to satisfy my curiosity about how much he really knew. This was not going to be easy. Roderick was popular, everybody know him. He was not a Curtis or a Rupert and could not be intimidated. He was more inclined to draw his old rusty cutlass from under the seat (every driver has one) and demand I get off his van.

I reach the old bus stop at Tèt Chimen sweating through my clothes. Two fellas were sitting in the shade sharing a joint. I said the usual good morning, which is your passport to new faces in the country, but they didn't answer; they never shift around on the roadside bench to make room for me. After standing long enough for them to grow accustom to me, I approach pretending to be casual, not looking at them in the eye. I ask the one nearest to me if he know where Roderick live. He look at me, up and down, taking time to absorb my face before he turn to his partner: "You know mate?"

The partner glance around, eying me up exactly like his friend: "Yo! Who you be, police or what?"

"He cyan be police, he would a make a move already." The

partner who I observe got salt-an'-pepper locks laugh hard like he just make a joke. "He waiting on transport like we."

"Think he got money?" the other one who look like a rude boy bellow.

"Money? We should a catch him last night before he find his crab hole. I sure the woman he fall asleep by drain his pocket dry; think she would let him go free?"

"Misyé? Take a good look at him, he not from here and he ain' got nada on him; sweet fock-all. That's how dem sagaboys from Castries stay. I not taking a dose a jail for stupidness. Let dat one alone." They speak for me to hear.

"I from here, I'm not a town boy," I said, itching to start a conversation. "I'm a policeman; a detective." I show them my badge. Both men shoot up to attention, you'd think they were on parade. "I not stopping you from smoking your joint; go on, blow your heads off, I'm investigating a murder."

"You is a detective, detective for what?" The rude boy laugh.

"I am investigating the murder of my sister. It happen up here, years ago. I can take you by my mother, Miss Agnes."

Both men were speechless. I could see them struggling to think what next to say. They were also trying to figure out if I was playing tricks on them. It take a while before the rude boy ask me: "You is Miss Agnes son for true?"

I look at him, smile, but didn't answer.

"My mother say he join police to find the man that kill his sister because he don' believe his father do it. I always think she was just talking..."

"Laurette is your sister?"

I get all excited when the salt-and-pepper locks guy speak about Laurette in present tense as if she still alive. I thought of correcting him, but I feel so good I stop short of telling him thanks. I didn't want to know their names in case I frighten them. At Bwa Nèf it's easy to frighten people that a few steps ahead of the law. The two seem slightly older than me but well beaten up by hard times.

The rude boy take a long draw on the spliff, his eyes stick to the floor. "She an' me was in the same class, your sister was a damn good-looking chick, I still cyan understand why a man had to go an' do her dat."

"Babylon got her father lock up, dey say is he kill her. Why dey still got dat man feeding all dem years in dere jail? Is either is he kill or he didn't kill, simple matter."

Salt-and-pepper locks seem far away, wrestling with a memory. "As far as I know dat case close long, we not hearing nothing 'bout it again."

"He's still on remand," I remind him. "The case is yet to call." Both men showed surprise.

"It must be hard to live wid a rope waiting to go round your neck," the salt-and-pepper locks partner remark.

"Nah! I think he innocent unless somebody can show me otherwise. I feel the authorities not too sure, because they doing nothing to close the case."

"Whaaat! Dis is serious shit you telling I man? Dat is human rights, block it right dere!" Salt-and-pepper locks look stunned. "All dem years dey lock up de man an' he can be innocent? Imagine dat? Never can tell wha going to happen when you bounce up with de squad an' dem. Dis place dangerous, Babylon again, Babylon day must come!"

"That's why I want to talk to Roderick. He was on the road; he can fill in some dots for me."

"How you self end up investigating your own case?" The rude boy ask.

"Who can do this better than me?"

"You know what time it happen? If it was in de morning and not in de night? You know if she did die in de house and he dump her under de bush." The rude boy was true to form. He remember the case but choose to fool around with me. Maybe he had a serious crush on Laurette, one he finds hard to shake off.

"I last see my big sister alive when she leave home to go by the seamstress. I was outside bathing; she knock me on my backside when she pass." I could feel them listening.

The locksman untied his tongue. "She was troublesome but if you is her friend she will talk to you but she must like you first." He pause to get my reaction before continuing. "What you think about your father? Why Babylon have him in dere jail if is not he dat kill your sister?" I couldn't answer him.

An engine rev up the steep slope below the lay-by like loaded with passengers. As it turn the bend both men shout: "Look him! Look Roderick." It was a good sign; the two guys turn on my side. They get up by habit and move to the edge of the curb to board the bus as soon as it park alongside the concrete platform. They wait until everybody collect their things, get off and pay. I hop on and sit next to Roderick. He did not recognise me; I put on a lot of size since my school days.

The two guys went to the long seat at the back of the van where they could stretch their legs. I could see them in the rear-view mirror looking at me. Roderick did not wait for more passengers; he did a three-point turn and swing his minivan around, driving back like a mad man, honking his horn at every bend. When he reach lower down by the signpost mark school zone, it was good timing to introduce myself. "I see you still the famous driver I use to know as a little boy, Mr Roderick."

He took his eyes off the road for a split second to look at me. His face did not show his age; he look younger than I predict.

"Why you say so?" he ask, smiling.

"Because I never stop hearing your name in my ears. My mother give you big ratings. She say you are the best driver this side of Dennery."

"Your mother know what she talking about, my boy." He grinned, flashing a gold cap in the left corner of his mouth. "You from here? I never see you before." Curiosity get the better of him.

I hesitate, smile, creating suspense. Lower down, an old woman standing near Paulinos rum shop signal him to stop. Roderick swing towards the curb, the old woman board and he continue on his way.

"How far you reaching?" Roderick ask her.

"Castries." That was all their conversation before he return to me. "And you, Mr Sweetmout, how far?"

"By the junction."

"Short trip, yes. Today every cent count, very little business on a Sunday."

I could not let this opportunity pass. "You know my mother," I said. "Miss Agnes?"

"Just now!" He raised his right foot off the accelerator and almost touch the brake. "You is the little boy she send to school in Dennery right after Lovence do what he do?"

Oh God! Here it goes again! I say to myself. "I don't know he do anything." I could feel a sharp edge in my voice.

"That's true, sorry, after all he's your father."

"How they calling you again? Names don't always stick in my head when I don't see you often."

"Andrew!" I lower my voice.

"Yes! Now you tell me I can see is you self. The face only get fatter."

"The little boy you drive to school on Monday mornings and bring back Friday evenings to his mother, that's me." I smile and shake my head.

"I sure all the time this was happening you didn't know was your father who kill your sister?"

"Up to now, I don't know."

"Don't say that, nobody will believe you."

"I swear; I am not sure. The court still has to decide." I was getting a little hot under the collar, my body start itching, my head get light from the heat inside the van, like when I drink too much beer. "You must not repeat everything you hear. You don't know when it's a bunch of lies." I was speaking loud above the sound of the engine. The three people on board heard and stick out their ears. "OK! OK! You very sensitive. As a policeman you bound to know more than me."

He knows all along I am a policeman but says nothing. He's a strange one. I can't help but begin to reassess Roderick. There is a secretive side to him, I am not sure if that is good or bad. "How you know I'm a policeman, but didn't know me when I come on board?"

"Up here, we smell you before you reach. All policemen smell like leather and polish. I know you was police before you enter the minivan."

He laugh but when he see I not laughing, he says, "Your mother tell me, and everybody else from the day you join the force."

"I am trying to understand certain things that never make any sense so I hope you don't mind if I ask you a few questions."

I could feel him thinking; he slow down the machine. "What questions?"

"Things like the morning my father hop your transport down the road to take him by his aunty?"

"Phew! Stale news! I speak to police; they ask me about that. That's so long ago." Roderick was shrugging me off politely, but I was not going anywhere.

"I read your statement. Your times were not too clear. In fact they were later than everybody else."

"Wha you mean?" He was not angry, a bit concerned though. "I take my time from the van. If it's not clear is what the van say." Although umpteen years pass, and a different van, it did not stop me peeping at my watch and glancing at the dashboard. There was a seven-minute difference. My watch was fast by five minutes, I keep it so to be on time for appointments. "Well let's start, I think, when you bounce up with Curtis and Rupert that morning?"

"Hah! You been checking on me?" He eye me in jest. "Everything you want to ask me the police know and write it down in their book and make me sign. If they lose the paper is not my fault."

I could see him beaming. For a second, I lose my composure. "Was there something between you and Laurette?"

He took his left hand off the steering wheel and pat my shoulder. "No!" he said quietly. "Something like what? Man and woman things? She was a child, a nice child, I don't interfere with children. I like her, she was quiet, but always afraid and looking over her shoulder."

"Afraid? Afraid of what? You sure?" This was important.

"She was my little friend, like her mother. When I meet Laurette walking up the road going by Miss Eldra, I would stop and pick her up. At first, not for hell I can get her to hop on, don' care how much passengers I have going to Tèt Chimen. She only start coming after Miss Agnes tell her it was alright. Something was after that child; you can't be always afraid, always looking over her shoulder and nothing wrong."

"I hear she was afraid of boys. Don't ask me why, although I suspect I know."

"Every time she put her foot in the van she looking back to see if somebody there watching her."

"Ever mention that to the police?"

"Me. Them fellas come up here looking for somebody to hold. That wasn't an investigation. I tell them what I know, and I done with that. Miss Agnes is my friend; I take her everywhere she want to go up to now. When she have money she does pay me. I never like how that man use to treat her. If she was my family, I done beat mate up and take a dose of jail."

Here it goes again, allegations, allegations.

"You think my father had anything to do with Laurette always being frighten?"

"How I can know the answer to that, I would have to be under the same roof."

"Laurette could tell you." I halt to take in his reaction, he look quite serious. "Who you think kill her?" I ask carefully picking my words.

"I can't help you." Roderick went on the defensive. "I was on the road from six to six that day. I get a trip to Vieux Fort; I eat there and get a chance to pee. You got to ask the officers that arrest your father, some of them still around. If they didn't know what they was doing, they should a leave him alone until they ready. You can't hold a man and feed him all these years in jail for nothing, especially when he got a wife and children. Why put them in hell too, and for nothing."

"I'm not here to trick you, only trying to find out the truth. It's important to get fresh information that can either clear my father's name or convict him." I could tell I was getting nowhere; maybe another angle would be more fruitful.

How Roderick and Mama manage to become friends is one puzzle I wanted to unravel, but how to do it without asking the hard questions was another problem. Mama was not one to ingratiate with other people so easy, especially men. She would consider Roderick a stranger and since he was not her husband or family, she would keep him far until Papa approve by telling her it was alright to speak to him. Roderick was not a neighbour and from what I gather has an obvious dislike for Papa.

"Driving up an' down the road in my van, taking you all to Health Centre in Dennery village and everywhere else that's how I get to know Miss Agnes." It's interesting he calls her Miss.

"You was too small. You had a bad cold that wouldn't leave you. Laurette was older, she would remember that if she was here. She use to carry you on her back when she come by the road. You was too heavy for her shoulders. Your little brother come long after that.

"From the minute your Mama arrive and she sit in her little corner 'til she reach her destination, not a word unless you talk to her," he said. That was Mama alright, quiet, different from the rest. I learn from him Laurette was getting to be like her — already they started to look alike. You had to open her mouth to get her to talk.

"There have some people — I can't tell you why — you just staying so an' like them. Me and Miss Agnes, like that." I could see his eyes getting red like he wanted to cry.

There was no reason to believe they were more than good friends and it was clear from Roderick's tone, Mama trust him.

Roderick was talking to me more than in all his interviews with detectives and it was interesting. But was he helping me solve this puzzle? That was another matter I had to consider fast.

"What about Curtis and Rupert? They were on board your van that morning, of course." I switch lanes back to the question I had asked Roderick earlier and which he sidestep deliberately or not.

"Check your records, man, it all there at the station." Roderick was getting riled up and fighting to disguise it. "I meet Curtis waiting by Paulinos rum shop. I take him up the road. Rupert was by the bus stand at Tèt Chimen waiting exactly where I pick you up, shaking like a wet leaf that heavy with dew; it look like he was looking for a shot. Curtis and Rupert ride with me all the way to Dennery. They tell me they want to go Castries, but I was not going that far. Somebody had book me for a trip to the airport in Vieux Fort from the day before and I was not going to let that money pass."

"Don't they live together and always together? How come on that morning they separate?"

"Police had them inside for months but let them go. They must be ask them those questions, I can't answer for them."

Roderick begin to accelerate as the road straighten into long stretches, but I was not finished. "What time you pick up Curtis?"

"About half past eight. I remember because we reach Dennery village before school start. I see the children playing in the schoolyard, so I know my timing right on that one."

"Good, and you say Rupert was with him?"

"What you trying? Yes, yes, they were going to Castries."

"I'm sorry. I wasn't trying to trick you or anything. It's hard to think straight in a moving vehicle."

"The way you on top of things? I say you are an expert. If it was not you, I done make the person asking me all this foolishness get down from my van." He flex his muscles and hold on to the steering wheel with both hands showing he was in charge. "Laurette was like my little sister, I never have one. That's all there was between us. If those two had made the mistake to kill her you would not meet them around still. Trust me."

I could feel him angry, trying to agree on whether to continue the conversation; but he chose to continue. "After I come back on my first trip to Dennery, Lovence was walking up the road. He flag me and ask to drop him by his aunty, Miss Eldra. It had to be close to eleven, because after that I leave for Vieux Fort with the people that hire me."

"So you only saw my father when you get back, about eleven, not before? I don't suppose you remember what he told you?"

Roderick laughed; it was a hearty laugh. "You trying to make me confess? I just tell you he ask me to take him up the road by his family. When I reach in front Miss Eldra house he ain't show sign he want to get down so I take him higher up to the bus stand at Tèt Chimen. He pay me for the short trip. I will not charge Miss Agnes, but not him."

(Miss Eldra? It struck me nobody ever interviewed her. Another sign of incompetence. She's gone now, too late for me to correct that error, but I can try talking to her daughters, they might remember something not yet on file.)

"How did he look, nervous, or what? Did he have stains on his clothes?"

"What I looking in the man face for, or care if his clothes clean or dirty, that's for his wife to see."

My suspicions were confirmed; every time my father surface in the conversation, Roderick gets furious. Could it have to do with Mama? Was Papa in his way? I merely asking myself.

"Every little thing helps me to understand what took place that morning, so go easy with me, I was a child."

Roderick went quiet, but underneath he was working himself up into a fit. His eyes dance in his head, I could swear he was seeing Papa again that morning in his van. "You know he had a postcard picture of Laurette showing off at Paulinos, boasting about his daughter and how he sending her to England to be a nurse as soon as she finish school."

"Never hear about that one."

"I never see the picture myself, but I hear talk on the van."

"What you think?"

"Laurette look like Miss Agnes, she had her face and he could see that."

"Explain? I am lost."

"If you don't catch what I saying find a new job, police work not for you. Laurette young and resemble her mother, make two and two stretch to eight. Think of what passing thru the man mind." If this can be corroborated as much as it is circumstantial, it would count as another nail in Papa's coffin. I want to ask more questions, but at this point it was not wise to show too much interest in the photograph, so I change the subject again: "He never tell you he was looking for Laurette, or ask if you see her that morning?"

"The man not my friend, he not going to ask me questions!"

"This has nothing to do with whether you friends or not. What would you do if it was you who can't find your daughter? She not at home and not in school where she supposed to be?"

"What you trying to say, he did know Laurette was dead? That man so full of tricks you can never tell." Something is not right; I must rework my notes before I go any further. I ask Roderick to stop. I need to take some pressure off my nerves. Everything's too convenient, textbook answers and I am none the wiser.

"We don' reach the junction and I know you ain't finish with me yet." Roderick glanced at me sideways with a half-smile.

"I will walk back from here to settle my mind." I was feeling a bit dizzy; not motion sickness but close to it.

"You bringing back things I want to forget, making me feel..." I didn't hear his last word, but the wrinkles on his face speak for him. He was sad.

Roderick stop under a mango tree; I could see ripe fruit scatter all over the road. I pay him and wave to the two characters in the back of the van who must have heard every word of our conversation but somehow that didn't seem important. Roderick did not want to take money from me, but I force him. Then begin a long slow walk up the road thinking about everything I learn since I start this investigation, only to realise up to that minute, I know nothing at all.

When I went back to work on Monday morning my first line of business was to tell Sarge about my meeting with Roderick and ask about the picture of Laurette. I thought it would be hard to bring up the subject, afraid there was some new skeleton waiting for me to discover, but it prove easier than I thought. Sarge had heard that story before and confirm Laurette was looking a lot like Mama when Mama was her age, as her body start to shape like a woman. "Check the exhibits, you'll see his passport, there's a picture of Laurette in it, I think it's the one Roderick tell you about."

I couldn't wait to go down to the exhibits room and search for myself. I didn't have to dig too deep before I find a full bleed picture of Laurette in black and white, postcard-size in Papa's passport, like Sarge said. Why was I not surprised?

# Chapter
## 8

Papa did not have money to fight his case but after fourteen years of struggle he was assigned a serious young lawyer willing to defend him pro bono or so he presented himself. (Sarge mention that an international organisation was footing the new counsel's bill and it was not true to say he was working for free.) He was much better than the court-appointed ones who were usually fresh from law school and would appear — only to disappear after each hearing. His first appearance on behalf of Papa before the judge was on grounds that it was cruel and inhuman to keep a man in custody away from his wife and family for fourteen years, seven months and two days without a trial and demanded bail be granted immediately. Mama sign away all her worldly riches to act as surety and give the court to hold the receipt for her house — the land was not hers.

Bail hearing was in the judge's chambers. Mama come to town dressed up in her Sunday best, smelling of kuskus grass and camphor balls. She pass by my home early and Angel give her a touch up, sprayed her from head to toe with a soft-smelling perfume to cut the strong armoire smells. I accompany her to the courthouse. The young lawyer said it would be a mere formality and Papa would be released in her care until the trial. Mama was beaming like I never see her before; the light make-up Angel arrange to highlight her eyes and accentuate her lips shave years off her face. The judge was one of those strict no-nonsense lady judges, who directed that only the lawyers involved should appear before her in chambers. Lovence had to remain in prison. Mama didn't seem to mind; the thought of getting her husband back consoled her. I sat with her on the bench outside the judge's chambers and waited. The director of public prosecutions went in with Papa's lawyer, who stop by for a brief chat with Mama. "They about to call your matter, we shouldn't be more than half an hour."

Mama smile and make a sign of the cross. Her day of deliverance had come.

Sergeant Willius pass by in full uniform to give us moral support and assure Mama it was going to be easy sailing. "The mere fact the matter is in chambers and not in open court mean you seeing your husband soon."

"Why I can't see him today?"

"Patience. There are a lot of papers to sign, the prison to be notified; your lawyer is very good at that, trust me." Mama was single-minded. All she wanted was to go back home with Lovence. "Why I still have to wait?"

"Not for long. If the judge say yes, I'd say by latest tomorrow afternoon." Sarge stay a while chatting but he had another issue to attend and left before Papa's matter was decided.

A jubilant attorney surfaced from the judge's chambers almost on the hour waving a pink sheet of paper. "I got bail." He spoke to Mama, smiles all over his face.

"When can we see him?" The words came out of my mouth without knowing.

"He is being released on surety signed by your mother; the court has his passport in evidence. He is not to be out after nine at night and to report to Dennery Police Station every Monday until the case is called." Mama hugged him, her eyes full of tears. "Thank you, thank you." The strain was too heavy to bear. She dropped back on the bench and cried her usual crop of tears.

The first night Papa get out from prison, he sleep by relatives in Castries. He did not go home until the next day. I stayed far away from him.

With Papa out on bail and the trial imminent, I start panicking. I was reading everything on file over and over hoping something unusual would catch my eye. Timelines, Sarge remind me, can be used to exonerate. In this case they were all over the place without creating a pattern. One witness claimed to catch a glimpse of Laurette crossing the road when he come from helping Mr Lucius ring the church bell for morning mass, but didn't mark the time, nor remember what clothes she had on. When asked by investigators some six months after giving his first statement Mr Lucius admit in writing: "I don't remember asking for help to ring the church bell that morning." There is no evidence of follow up and I could not find one person to help me locate the individual who claim he assisted Mr Lucius that morning. My exercise looked futile. I could not point out any one person who was seen under the bush around the same time Laurette left Miss Claire's place that fateful morning.

It was like looking at a jigsaw puzzle; bits and pieces all over the place. Not enough men had been assigned to this case in the early stages and important leads slipped through the cracks. Statements were taken from witnesses without names or addresses and left on file, forgotten and useless. In some instances, investigators lost contact when parties move away from Bwa Nèf. Several people died, including one justice of the peace. I work through the mess, leaning heavily on Sergeant Willius as my pilot, apprehensive, but zealous. I lament the levels of incompetence at all stages and believe this might be the real reason why my "friend", the corporal, did not want me around, and why a case against Papa could not be made sooner. I needed clues badly to point me in other directions. I had some names in my head like Fafan but nothing strong enough to give me confidence. Half of me is saying Papa did not do it when I look at mess in the files; the other half, well —

I read and re-read statements from Mr Lucius and Roderick. Both were asked to take off their shirts in the presence of a medical examiner and then let go. There was no note on file to indicate that they were suspects or persons of interest, nor were they cautioned, but they were still asked to bare their backs. Why not Papa? Mama was present every time Papa was called to the station so I was told. She is on record answering questions address to him while he's thinking of what to say. "Why interview them together?" Sarge didn't have an answer, all he could say was, the usual excuse, they were not suspects. "Of course, you can now appreciate the good police work your friend did." Sarge smile watching me swim in my own self-inflicted misery. "The mess you mean." He loves to refer to the corporal by his code name "Friend".

Sergeant Willius try to explain the glitches facing the prosecution, but only succeed in muddying the waters more. In my opinion it was shoddy police work. My family were poor country people that could not afford a good lawyer, and even Sarge, who I consider family, give me the impression at times he was on the bandwagon. Once, I pestered him about the lousy interrogation work and his response to me was: "Who brazen enough to suspect people in their grief?"

A fine thread keeps coming at me and will not go away. Something in the doctor's report: "If it is any consolation, she scratched him up left, right, and centre..." A question that couldn't be more obvious came to me, yet nobody could give a logical answer: how did Papa dress soon after the murder, especially for interviews with police?

Sarge said "Our Friend" observed that in the days and weeks following the murder, Papa always came to the station, whether in Dennery or Castries, neatly dressed in a white long-sleeve shirt, button down to the wrists and also had on a tie. "He look more like a lawyer than the lawyers," Sarge remarked.

"And nobody think to check him out for scratches?" I shake my head.

"He told me this long after your father was arrested." One look at Sarge, I could see he did not believe that the corporal observed anything, more than likely he was told.

"I never see Papa wearing a tie." I thought hard. Maybe he dress again somewhere else after he leave the house.

"He borrowed it," Sarge chip in. "For a man that mostly wear khaki why it didn't seem strange to detectives that he's dressing up like a lawyer every time he come to them? I can't say they were not aware of the evidence under Laurette's fingernails. Long-sleeve white shirt and tie, what for?" Sarge fumed. "And nobody find it suspicious."

I could feel him thinking of what next to say and when he did he gave a whole summary. "You had evidence, the scratches; you were looking for a man with marks on his back and chest, maybe on his face too, definitely his arms, his neck, his thighs — you've got pubic hairs — and in spite of all of this, you don't check the man who say he find the body?"

"The scars wouldn't they still be there six months later?" I asked, curious for confirmation.

"Christ man!" Sarge storm. "I don't know what the hell went on, but I can tell you it was ridiculous. I did what I could to bring him in on what we had but these guys were my seniors. You think I am not frustrated!"

"You brought him in six months after…"

"Better late than never."

"My sister put up a hell of a fight, records show. Don't tell me the corporal didn't know that too because he had Mr Lucius and Roderick take off their shirt and pants. He was on the right track following the evidence, yet the main man in all of that get a free pass; it's amazing!"

"That's your father you talking about!" Sarge tried to cool me down, but I was too hot under the collar to listen.

"A simple check could have spared us the misery we went through."

"It could have gone either way."

"At least he would not still be accused."

Sarge agreed. "I was only a little private watching the majòs do their work. He would come all button up to check on the status of the investigation and bringing fresh information on Curtis and Rupert, while they were in jail. Up to a day like today this long-sleeve white shirt thing eats me out. All of us felt sorry for your father and his wife until we realise he was a little too pushy trying to pin the crime on Curtis and Rupert with information we could not corroborate. Who send him to look for your sister? Who said she was missing? Your mother never tell us she did. Looking back, it's easy to see your mistakes when everything is laid out for you. Think about the poor detectives just getting this case piecemeal with only one or two men assigned to it."

I ask Sarge whether there was a picture of Papa wearing the shirt, or statements with a description; I wonder whether shots were taken by the press; they came early that afternoon. "We have pictures of the crime scene but nothing with your father except mug shots. None of the CID men pay attention to that side of the investigation, they were more concerned about processing the scene and going back to Castries."

Sarge said he remember asking senior detectives whether they took photographs of Papa soon after the murder and they told him it was not necessary as he was not a person of interest in the case. After some digging, I come across in a back issue of a local newspaper, pictures of Laurette's funeral and there's Papa in a long-sleeve shirt and tie in the cemetery shovelling dirt on the coffin.

"By the way," Sarge growl in his laid-back style when he think he got a surprise: "Don't waste much time on Laurette's picture, the parish priest took it at a church bazaar months before she died. I check that out early in the game. Your father was showing off."

"And only now you saying…"

"Just checking how far you would go." Frankly, I felt relieved.

I found the record of Papa's call from Tèt Chimen to Dennery Police Station at 11.17am to report he found his daughter dead under the bush near his house. Sergeant Willius was then a constable working the beat in Castries and did not know until he hear it on the evening news on his transistor radio next day. Nor did he get interested until he saw Mama in the papers and recognise her. From then on, he start keeping close to CID after telling them Mama was family and they allow him to hang around headquarters and feed him with bits and pieces.

As I find out more things about Papa's case, I went in my shell. I wasn't myself. My colleagues said my strange behaviour was because of Angel's pregnancy and the expectations of becoming a father. I was happy I did not have to explain the truth.

About two to three weeks after Papa come from jail, Angel give birth to a baby girl; she weighed seven pounds eight ounces. Angel come from hospital with the baby three days after confinement and went straight by her mother: "She at me until she learn how to feed and bathe the child properly." According to Miss Beatrice, Angel didn't know anything about man or child, she herself didn't give her no bopè and never look for more children after Angel was born.

Miss Beatrice was superstitious. Every Monday morning, she took a trip to the gadè to learn about her future and come back repeating some of the strangest things you could ever hear. The one miracle in her life the gadè never foresee to warn her was Angel having a baby girl. There was prediction Angel's first child was going to be a boy and Miss Beatrice dutifully drown herself in blue.

I remain alone for a month in our little two-room house and visit Angel and our baby after work. At nights my mind wander. There was always the moment when my thoughts go back to the day Papa find Laurette under the bush. I start seeing Laurette every night, alive and fresh in my mind, but looking very restless. I speak to a young priest after mass one morning and he tell me maybe she is unhappy. He recommend I give a mass for the repose of her soul. I give him ten dollars but I don't know if he said the mass because Laurette keep appearing more often than before I pay him, fresh, just like she was in the coffin, her face make-up like a big woman with rouge on her cheeks and lipstick on her lips and not a day older.

One night I was lying on the bed watching television, tired, listless, sleep not coming; on top of that, the electricity company then take the current and leave me in the dark. It's difficult for me to believe some of what happen is just coincidence, dreams so alive, they put reality to shame. Imagine, I by myself, pitch black, can't see my hands, yet I hear a fine, clear voice calling my name: "Andrew! Andrew! Andrew!" I could hear the breeze on the roof and a dog howling in the neighbour's yard. I put my head back down on the pillow, I can hear vehicles racing up and down the street. Then, I hear the fine clear voice again: "He kill me an' nothing for that."

I jump out of bed and bolt to the door. The key was in my pocket, I had not yet change into my pyjamas. I hesitate before turning the key in the lock, hoping to detect exactly where the voice coming from. I hear the dew on the galvanise above my head. Outside was damp. I prefer to remain inside, but shit scared to make that choice. This had everything to do with the way I was raised and the superstitions around me. I take the key out from the keyhole and put it back in my pocket and return to bed. But before I could rest my head down, the fine clear voice like an angel in the rafters come back again: "What you saying for that, Andrew, he can kill me?"

God! Please don't tell me I going off this time of night! I pinch myself, but I don't believe I feel anything. I turn the key in the lock again and find myself outside in a sweat. It was new moon; I was glad for the light. On the steps I listen to night sounds, anything to take my mind away and wait until the current come back.

I beg Miss Beatrice to please let Angel return with the baby. If I stayed by myself much longer, I would go mad. Miss Beatrice agree. She was sure Laurette was coming to help me and I must not chase her away. She fix an oil lamp and give it to me with one of her little statues of the Virgin Mary. She decide to say the prayers but I had to keep the oil lamp burning day and night until Laurette find peace and return to her resting place, which she believe was in purgatory. "She die before making a full confession. The *onliest* way she will go back is when they catch and hang the person that take her life. That's all she wants."

# Chapter
## 9

From the day I start my own investigations is Papa's name I want to clear. What I need most is a suspect, somebody apart from him that I can look at and say, yes! he did it. I been looking through the evidence with fresh eyes, but the more I dig, the more I realise is a deep hole I digging to bury Papa. All I am doing is trying to ease shame on the family; there was fear that a stain could attach itself to my name if Papa was found guilty. Should I get this right, new evidence can save him.

Among the statements I come across on file was one by Miss Philomene, our neighbour, who lives in the house closest to us. In it she stated she see when Laurette go up the road that morning around seven; it was after she send Fafan to the belfry to bring his grandfather's tea. (That would be Mr Lucius. Nobody ask her what time Fafan left with the tea.) Not much attention was paid to her statement because it read like everybody else and was ignored by investigators including me, until now. Nevertheless, it place Fafan on the road about the same time as Laurette. Miss Philomene should have been asked how long after Fafan left with the tea that Laurette pass. What if he stop somewhere on the road and they meet? That's crucial in relation to what happen later. However, Fafan never said he met her on his way to his grandfather. It was on his return home.

Miss Philomene had gone senile and did not remember the days of the week, but I could talk to her daughter, Miss Pinky. More than ever, I needed Fafan's address. I think my mind was fixed on finding a scapegoat to get Papa out of the calaboose and Fafan was the person I pick. So I went to interview Miss Pinky.

She did not invite me into the house like Miss Claire but leave me standing outside while she look down over her windowsill as if I just stop by for a casual hello. Miss Pinky was not clear on anything about what her mother told her so I had to do a lot of prompting. When police spoke with her mother, two days after Laurette's death, she still had a good head on her shoulders according to Miss Pinky. In her statement, Miss Philomene said she saw Laurette with a black plastic bag in her hand. This helps to corroborate other statements particularly by Miss Claire, who remembered it was about half past seven when Laurette came to her house with her uniform in a black plastic bag. No sense repeating the same things over and over, Miss Pinky offered nothing new but was able to give me Fafan's address off an envelope with a card from last Christmas.

So what I know was that Laurette was alive when she leave the seamstress house and cross the high road on her way back to get ready for school. This was between 7.30am and 8.00am. Knowing Laurette, she had to be in a hurry. She love school and never want to be late, not once. It would not take her ten minutes from the high road to home. What happen between leaving the high road and reaching the hill by our house is crucial; it is certain she was killed within that narrow window in time.

I went back to the statement by Fafan taken two days after the murder. It makes interesting reading. Don't forget he lived close by, the same distance like us from the main road. We must pass in front of their house to get out of the gap. They hear everything happening on the hill above them where we live: if we speak in our sleep or when we scream from Mama's whippings.

What Fafan had to say puts things in some perspective: "I live with my grandmother Miss Philomene at Bwa Nèf, by where Laurette living with her mother, her brother Andy and a little brother. I know Laurette, we go to the same school. Every morning before the sun get up my grandfather does leave to go ring the church bell for the priest before he goes in the pasture to cut grass and give his cow water. My grandmother does wake up to make his tea and send me to bring it for him. I leave about half past seven to bring his tea every morning. I meet my grandfather by the church; I give him the tea and wait until he finish to give me back the basket and the flask to go home. I had to get ready for school. I don't see Laurette on the road when I was going, only when I was coming back. She pass me in the gap running to her house. Before I could ask her anything, she gone. She doesn't talk to boys like that. Her father will beat her if he catch her talking to boys. It was about eight o'clock when I see her. I don't see Laurette again on the road when I leave to go to school and I did not see her at school."

His statement confirms a few things I already know — Laurette never reach home to dress for school that day and Fafan, according to the register, was lying. He never made it to school. Probably he was attempting to hide his truancy, yet clear as it was the investigators never followed that line. They accepted his statement without asking questions. The part where he write: "…she doesn't talk to boys like that. Her father will beat her if he catch her…" send me to the drawing board. How he know that? Did she tell him? When? I never see Papa beat any one of us.

Questions buzz through my head; the noise get louder when I study what Laurette's class teacher had to say to police. He mention she was always frightened about something (Roderick said the same thing). Even in class, he could not get her to open her mouth and answer questions far less on a private matter which the teacher believe had something to do with home. "She will just sit in class and dream." I could see him fighting the tears. Laurette was still fresh in his memory.

Here is what I find relevant in his statement: "Laurette was not a backward child but behaved like she was stupid. I am the only male teacher at the school, and she showed she was afraid of me. All the other teachers who taught her before said she was bright, but I can't say so because her mind was never in the classroom. I believe now her problems were much deeper than just boys. But it was not until after she died, I came to realise maybe she lived in fear of her father." Her teacher was young, fresh from college but with common sense to spot that something was wrong. But why jump on Papa? Did he leave out something because he did not want to incriminate somebody? Is he writing one thing but thinking something else? More questions, more roads to follow.

When I spoke to Miss James, the old principal, who had retired and moved to the village to be close to the sea and her church (she claims sea baths ease the rheumatism in her knees and was groaning every second I spend with her). She remembered Laurette clearly and found her reserved, clever (the exact word she use) but, she added, "this was not immediately apparent unless you spoke to her. Some boys thought she was fresh, but when she died they came together and carried her coffin from the hearse to the church and from the church to the cemetery without me having to ask them. They even cried, some of them."

All that was good but I wanted to know more. "You remember a boy name Fanis Jules, nickname Fafan?"

"Of course. Yes, he was popular with all the girls in his class. A real showman."

"He was in same class with my sister?"

"I don't think so. If I recall, he was a bit older."

"They were good friends though?"

"I would not be surprised. That boy was always showing off and the girls liked it; you know at that age everything is pappy show."

"I am going to ask you a question, not that I know anything but because I want to understand Laurette a bit more."

Miss James fix her face in a corkscrew to look at me. I can hear her saying inside, "Careful little boy, you too young to try and fool me."

"Did Laurette have a crush on Fafan?"

"I can tell you straight off, no. Maybe it was the other way around. He organise the boys in his class to carry the coffin without me asking." Tears came to her eyes. I had a few more questions to ask. She saw me hesitate. "You not finished with me yet, young man, ask away, if it will help bring peace and closure to you."

My eyes flash on to the brown rosary beads wrap round her wrist. Feeling bold, I press home some more questions about Fafan. "Was he at school that day? Was he late? Did he have any scratch marks on him?" I did not want to raise Teacher James' blood pressure so I thought if I asked her everything one time it would be a lot easier for her to answer.

She looked at me smiling. "How you expect me to remember all this? Tell you what though, go to the parish priest, ask him to show you the school register. That will help you much better than this old memory." We continued with some small chat before I left her alone.

At this stage, going through my notes and hoping to find nuggets

I overlook had me depressed. Things were not falling in place as fast as I wanted — not until I went back to Roderick remarks. "I pick up Curtis by the rum shop, he was waiting for me; it was about eight thirty and I drive up the road where I meet Rupert, he was trembling like he sleep under the bush and he cold; he ask me for a cigarette. I don't smoke. I take both of them to Dennery town."

Why was Rupert trembling at the bus stop that morning, sun up and burning hot already? I don't think it was rum he wanted; something he see got him frighten. Or something he did and it stick on his conscience. He is not the kind of man to stay quiet and take blame for other people. Perhaps that morning Rupert was sick, or it was earlier than Roderick believe and still cold outside. One thing I gather through experience, when it comes to time, an eyewitness without a watch is unreliable.

There were days Mama have Laurette stay away from school to help her, like when Marvin fall sick, which was often; she would send her down to the river to wash his diapers, or run errands by Mr Paulinos. I don't know if Papa hang around the house on those days, he could, not having a fixed job. Sometimes, I remembered, he help Miss Grainy — she's gone now, bless her soul.

I never know what he did for her until I read her statement. "I reach by Lovence house after nine o'clock, about half past. I see Lovence brushing his teeth by his kitchen, under the standpipe outside. He was bareback in his kalson and it look like he was cleaning himself. I speak with him. I tell him Curtis and Rupert not coming to help me today; I did tell them I would not be there. I want him to cut down a kannèl tree for me. He come with his cutlass about ten o'clock, he cut the tree and leave. He had on a khaki short pants and white long-sleeve shirt, button up to his neck. I did not see no scratch on Lovence when he was bathing. Doctor say I can see close but not far, I got cataract in both eyes. I don' see no scratch on his face when he come to cut the tree for me, but I wasn't looking for scratch."

"White long-sleeve shirt, button up to the neck." Either Miss Grainy got the time wrong, mixing up the days in the week, not forgetting it was six months after the incident when detectives took her statement, or she was the only one spot on, give and take half an hour. I did not see her on the road when I went by Miss Claire to look for Laurette, or on my way back to school. Miss Grainy's timeline of half nine was reasonable; I could not meet her at half past nine, I was in school. If she was in the gap earlier, I would hear her shouting Miss Philomene to let her know she is around. Papa arrive on her land at about ten, she said, which was half an hour from the time she speak to him, not time enough in my books to wash off marks — scratches — and erase suspicion in the minds of detectives. He come with his cutlass knowing full well what he come and do, yet he put on his Sunday best, the only white long-sleeve shirt in his trunk. He's not the one washing it so he's not afraid it get stain? Or is he hiding something under the long sleeves?

Investigators had a chance to pounce on that statement no matter it was six months late; they had seen the autopsy report which mention about skin under Laurette's fingernails. Those at the scene see the doctor collect and bag evidence from under her nails — that must tell you there could be scratches on the suspect. Listening to Mama, I get to know Papa wear this long-sleeve white shirt twice before that: at Laurette's first communion and for Marvin's christening. My mind race into overtime. Why wear it now? Come on, detectives, think. This thing bother me for weeks until I sum it up in one word — incompetence.

My process of elimination began with an open mind while I follow Sarge's advice to a tee and keep to myself. The investigators place their last dollar on Rupert and Curtis being the culprits without paying attention to anything else. They lost big time and throw their hands in the air letting the investigation slide away from them. However, there was one matter I needed to clear in my mind concerning Rupert.

Rupert saw something, I had the feeling, a sixth sense, something so terrible it tie his tongue. What is it Rupert see to turn him speechless? Why he so ready to take jail rather than speak? Probably it was connected to the indecent assault case weeks before the murder. Papa insist they were guilty; you'd think he catch them red-handed. He travel up and down to Dennery station until both men were arrested. The case file show Papa as the complainant and Laurette the sole witness. I could not find the actual police report on the incident; it may be misfiled in all the excitement that come after. Mama say there were scratches on Laurette's shoulders and breasts, enough to show where somebody grab her and she fight back, but I could find no medical evidence to support that. Mama did not take her to the doctor as instructed. Instead, she full Laurette with turmeric tea, morning and night until she believe she drank enough. In any case, with little or no evidence it was easier to drop the matter, more so since the key witness was dead.

With intention of killing two birds with one stone, I picked a weekday to go up to Bwa Nèf: to see the parish priest about the school register and afterwards make a social call on Rupert. Father Jonas Sylvester was a young priest acting for the parish priest who had gone to France on family matters. I came up on a transport making sure it was not Roderick's. I did not want to be seen, and got off below Miss Claire at the junction where a side road takes you to the church and the presbytery next door. Being a local, Father Jonas was familiar with Laurette's story and showed surprise when I told him the case was not called after all this time. He express regret for the absence of the district registrar who had gone off on maternity leave, leaving him all alone to find his way. He seemed to have caught on quick and returned with a handful of registers for standards four, five and six for 1998. I had given him the date, so while I went through standard four, he shuffled through five and six.

I came to the page for September 11 — the names were in alphabetical order. I raced down the page to S and trembled when I saw Laurette Stephen in a legible handwriting, blue ink. Register columns marked present or absent were ticked appropriately, except next to her name. There was no indication if she was there or not; it was as if she did not exist. On further examining the register, I discover Fanis Jules was in standard six. He did not attend school that week from Wednesday, which was the 9th. Somebody had entered "Absent due to illness" on the Friday next to his name, the same day Laurette died. He was back in school the following Monday and off again the Thursday. In fact, every week from January he took at least one day off from school. I thanked the priest for his help and swore him to secrecy sealing the deal with a crisp new purple twenty-dollar bill.

Rupert was not so easy a proposition. As expected, he was cagey and insisted on Curtis being there while I speak to him. I recited a whole litany on how sorry I was about what happened to them earlier on and lied a little about how my sergeant and I went to great lengths to make sure they were not bothered again on any matter concerning Laurette. I don't know if he believe me because he kept asking for a piece of paper to show. After I feel that Rupert and Curtis were comfortable with me coming inside their little kabé and sitting on the dirt floor with them, I start with my questions. "I hear the morning Laurette die there have people that say they see you up the road trembling."

"Ah! Who say so?"

"People. It's not important now. Nothing can happen to you, not after your name has been cleared. It's up to you if you choose to go and commit yourself somewhere else."

"I trying hard to go straight. Curtis and I makin' coals at Gwan Bwa and take to town to sell."

We play cat and mouse for almost an hour, all the while Curtis there listening, then I say again: "I need to know what get you so frighten that morning your teeth couldn't stop clapping against one another." Without prompting Curtis open his mouth: "Well tell de man, you didn't do noffing."

Rupert look at Curtis under the eye as if to say what nonsense yourself talking. I can tell they were close, like in a husband-and-wife way, and had each other's back. I could feel Rupert softening, not the bèt sovaj I make him out to be. I needed to give him an incentive to talk; it was just after pay day and I still had a few dollars in my pocket so I offer him twenty dollars and promise to keep whatever he said in confidence.

His eyes light up. It didn't seem he make that much money in a long time. He whisper something to Curtis that I didn't hear. Then he look at me straight. "Twenty for me, an' twenty for Curtis."

I did not hesitate, couldn't take a chance with him changing his mind. I dive into my wallet and take out two bills. "I got the money for you, so now don't give me no cock and bull; you know I can tell if you speaking the truth."

"If we did have a little someting to go down de throat dat would be nice," Curtis chirp in. These two are a real tag team, penny and two cents, they can read one another's mind.

"Nothing until I hear what Rupert got to say and he better come strong."

Rupert start with one long preamble about every morning as the sun come over the hill how he does get up and go to the bush to do his business, the way he describe it was funny but I couldn't afford to laugh. "Curtis does be sleeping still when I go out." He tell me there's a special pear tree by itself, and when you climb it you can see Miss Grainy land and all the way down hill by the ravine. It not too far from our house, he said. "Is not a road people use often but you can pass dere to go straight to Tèt Chimen from your place."

He was on top the tree doing his business looking down the ravine. "The water was clear and I could see de sun washing it face in de basen."

Then, he says, he hears like a scream that freeze every bone in his body. The scream sound like it come from the ravine. He try to see the place where the scream come from but bush bar him, and he only see a piece of the road going uphill but nothing going down to the ravine and by Miss Philomene house. He hear the scream again — this time it sound like a pig you stab in the neck to slaughter. He pull up his pants and slide down the tree and forget the leaves he take to clean himself. He was thinking what to do when he see a man in khaki short pants climbing the hill to go to our house. When the man almost reach he stop and go back down like he change his mind. "I don' know if he see me an' was comin' for me. I run like a mongoose through de bush all de way to de lay-by to wait for Curtis."

I stay stun for a while, the first words to come from me were: "What time was that?"

"Dis man is a joker, Curtis. If you hear an' see what I see, is time you gon to check?"

The most obvious question: I was afraid to ask it.

At last, I was beginning to see a light in what I set out to do. I had names for people that was under the bush when Laurette pass back from the seamstress on her way home. First I establish the timeline between eight and eight thirty. I know Rupert was there and saw something, whether he tell me everything is another matter, but he was there and heard enough to scare the skin off his back. Fafan was there, too, according to his statement: "When I was coming back she pass me in the gap running to her house."

Here is the hard one, whether I want to accept it, but Papa had to be there. He leave home before me, nobody see him by the road around eight and eight thirty that morning, I did not meet him in the two trips I make between home and the high road. Where did he go? The only explanation he give is he was at home all the time in the kitchen and left after I went to school. Mama says the same thing. However, he did not seem to know I came back to tell Mama that Laurette was not at Miss Claire, and that is what make me realise I know what I was saying all the time. Papa was not at home at all after I bathe and dress for school. Going back to Rupert, I believe he was telling the truth when he said he saw a man going up the hill to our house. Pure intuition tell me that was Papa, the way Rupert describe him. He know the person but afraid to say who. I think he put two and two together with the scream and that frighten him even more.

I wrote Fafan a nice letter asking him what he remember about my sister and if he could add anything more to the statement he made to police about the day she died. I also attach a photocopy of his statement to jog his memory and send everything by registered mail but never got a response. (I understand he writes to his mother; Mama tell me she goes sometimes to Castries to Western Union and does ask her to cast an eye on Miss Philomene until she get back.) I ask Sarge about my options and he insist let sleeping dogs lie. That didn't stop me writing Fafan again, this time by aerogram. Nothing doing, still no reply; I search on social media, his name does not appear; it could be he's there illegally working under a fake ID.

Here I was on my own working off the books, without Sarge. This was a delicate matter. I had to be careful that I didn't cause problems between Mama and Miss Pinky. They were friends although a little wobbly. I had to dig. I made a list of boys in Laurette's class and above and began eliminating potential suspects by a method only I understood. There were thirty-four names in all, scattered all over the place: fourteen were out of state, two in jail and one had died. How can I pursue those that are still around without my superior officer getting to know? A tough one, but I can't give up.

# Chapter
## 10

Marvin ring me one afternoon from Dennery Police Station crying. He was lucky to catch me at my desk; I just finish a report and getting ready to leave for the day. "Papa beat Mama so bad she's in the hospital."

"Oh God!" All that could come from my mouth was: "Where?"

"Dennery Hospital!" Marvin shout into the mouthpiece.

"Where's Papa?" I was furious.

"He home. I tell Mama I making a report but she tell me no, don' go. They will just take Papa and put him back in jail. She don' want that to happen."

"That's where he got to stay," I said. I could hear Marvin hiccupping; he must have been crying non-stop.

"She say if I call the police for Papa, she will tell them he didn't beat her. I don' know what to do. The corporal give me the phone to call you."

I ask Marvin to put Corporal Jn Pierre on the line. "Andy! Is me, I have a problem with this domestic violence matter involving your mother. Your brother is here to make a report but he tell me your mother will not cooperate. What you want me to do?"

"Take the report on a sheet of paper, don't enter it yet. I coming down. I will talk to Mama then tell you what to do."

"I can't hold back for long as you know. I will have to investigate and make an arrest."

"Just wait till you hear from me. I coming now." He pass the phone back to Marvin and I ask him to wait for me at the station and don't go back up to the house.

As soon as I arrive at the bus stand I was lucky to get transport on the peg going to Vieux Fort. One hour and a half later I was on Dennery Main Street. It was after six and beginning to get dark. I meet Marvin sleeping on a bench at the station. My friend Corporal Jn Pierre had finished for the day but it was nice of him to wait and keep my brother company. We stop by Mr James' bakery — I remember the shop from school days — and bought two loaves and a soft drink for Marvin. I ask him if he wanted anything in the bread. He said no and we continue on our way to the hospital. Corporal left us and went home but told me, if anything, stop by before I return to Castries.

On entering the ward I identify myself. The nurse said that Mama's eyes were bloodshot from a hard blow to the back of her head, maybe with an iron bar or a piece of very hard wood. Mama's head was bandaged, and the nurse had her hooked up to two bottles of drip on a stand next to her bed. She was sleeping, but when she hear my voice talking to the nurse, she wake up. "Andy! Andy! Is you?"

"Yes, Mama, is me. What happen to you?"

"Where Lovence?" She was asking me for her husband, the same man who send her to hospital.

"Marvin and me are here."

"She suffered a concussion," the nurse said. "Don't let her talk too much, she must not get excited."

"How you feeling Mama?" I could see both her eyes were black and swollen. She squinted to open them.

"I knock my head on the kitchen step." Marvin made me a sign, that's not true.

"Marvin there with you?"

"Yes, Mama, right by me." She was conscious and thinking. I was not certain if she could see well. I was hoping the blow did not blind her.

"Marvin, remember what I tell you en! Don't go to the police."

"I am here, Mama, I am the police." I answered for Marvin.

"You don't count, you is my child." Mama was conscious alright and know what she was about.

"Can you see, Mama?"

"I not blind yet," she snapped back.

"If you fall from the kitchen to the step and nobody push you that's an accident. Why you afraid if police know about it?"

"Is not me," she said and started to cry. "Is what they will say. Is what they will do."

"Why you crying, Mama? Something hurting you?" I try to calm her, but that only make her hysterical. She pull herself away and didn't want me to touch her.

"They will come an' arrest Lovence and say is he who hit me, I did not fall. That's their habit. They always blaming him for things he don' do, like they doing with Laurette. They see he don' have nobody to stand for him, they taking advantage; the man only going from lawyer to lawyer and for what? For nothing!"

Looking at her lying on the bed, still making excuse, I shake my head knowing she was giving Papa another break. She'd rather die than admit. I had to be very tactful how I approach this; it was no longer only between Papa and Mama; Marvin and I were involved. This situation cannot continue — they must live apart, or somebody going to get killed.

Mama notice that I gone quiet ask: "What you thinking about, Andy? I know you thinking."

I wave my hand across her face without touching her. "I see you fighting to open your eyes."

"No, is nothing," Mama whisper. A lightning bolt shoot up my spine, the rage in my stomach boiling hot.

Marvin couldn't take it anymore. I could see that from the look on his face. I hadn't bothered him for details at the station, the poor boy look shaken; but I wanted to hear what Mama had to say first.

It was not easy to watch Mama with puff eyes, head bandaged, lying on a hospital bed. Every ounce of pity I had for my father, drain out from my veins, especially when I watch Mama cry. However, knowing her and her denials, I can't afford to be reckless — his shit smell like perfume to her. He was first in everything, first to eat, first to have his clothes iron, shoes polish, bathe, sleep, and wake. We, her children, come after him in everything and she last.

I beg the nurse to follow me outside for a minute; I wanted answers to a few questions. The nurse said that when Mama was admitted, the doctor asked if somebody reported the matter to the police. "She receive a bad blow to the head, how she manage to walk is a miracle, but yet that's not enough to go to the police." The nurse spoke with a blank face, careful not to show her feelings. "The X-ray will tell us more in the morning. For now, you must let her rest," and she flashed one of her fancy official nurse smiles at me and I melt under the weight.

In times like this to say my head was hot would be an understatement. I didn't know what to do next. I call Sergeant Willius from the hospital; he was at home. He asked me to return to Dennery Station right away with Marvin and help him write his statement for the front desk. "This thing is escalating, you don't want another death in your family, you can't afford it, not right now, funerals not cheap."

"Sarge, you read my mind."

Marvin believe Mama would want to beat him for going to the police when she come out of hospital. I tell him he was not a child anymore. "You not going back to stay at that house, I will talk to my nennenn and leave you with her in Dennery until we can settle this matter. I will go up home with you first thing in the morning to get your clothes." Poor Marvin had no choice.

We return to Castries late, well past ten in the night. Marvin sleep with me, and in the morning we went back to Dennery after a stop by Angel's mother to let them know what happen. Angel insist I take care of Marvin until Mama was well again. I pass by the CID to see Sergeant Willius. He order me to take the rest of the week off as this was an emergency. We went straight back to the police station to brief Corporal Jn Pierre at the front desk. He agreed to detail a uniform officer to accompany us in the jeep to Bwa Nèf when we ready.

I ask Corporal to take an official statement from Marvin and help him write it. Marvin used the ballpoint chained to the counter and start slow as if trying to get his hand accustomed to the shape, starting with the date: 'My name is Marvin St Mark, I live at Bwa Nèf in Dennery. I reach home from Dennery village yesterday about four o'clock in the afternoon. I meet my mother Agnes Steven quarrelling with my father Lovence St Mark in the kitchen. I say good afternoon Mama, good afternoon Papa, they did not answer me. I go inside the house and change to my house clothes. I accustom hearing my mother and father quarrelling. Since my father come back home, they always quarrelling. After I put on my house clothes, I was standing in the bedroom door waiting for them to finish before I go in the kitchen. I hear my mother say something to my father that make him mad and he hit her twice with a piece of post he had in his hand and give her a gòjèt and throw her out in the yard. I see when he push her and she land on her head. Papa walk out from the kitchen, jump over her lying down on the ground and go down the hill. I believe Mama was dead, I did not know what to do. I try to lift her up but she was too heavy. I go in the kitchen and take a cup and full it with water from the pipe. I hold her head and try to make her drink from the cup.

"When I see nothing was happening, I run by Ma Philomene house to tell her daughter Miss Pinky that my mother take a bad fall in the yard. She leave what she was doing right away and come with me. My mother get up, we meet her sitting on the kitchen step. Miss Pinky ask me to get my shoes and wait for her in the kitchen and she take my mother inside the house. I hear them talking and I smell bay rum. Miss Pinky come back outside and tell me my mother got a bad headache and I will have to take her to hospital. I tell her I will go and call my father but she say not to worry about him. I see Mama lying down on the bed holding her head and crying. Miss Pinky wrap a serviette round her head like a bandage; not long after that Miss Pinky come back with Mr Lucius. I know him, he does ring the bell in church. My mother say he use to be Miss Philomene boyfriend and is Miss Pinky father. He also is teacher Merle father, Miss Claire last daughter."

I ask Marvin to take out the last part, it was not important. He was going to, but Corporal tell me to let him speak his mind, he would fix it afterwards.

Marvin continue: "My mother was trembling to walk; I hold the grip with her clothes, Miss Pinky and Mr Lucius help her reach by the road. We wait a long time for transport, but Mr Roderick come, he take us to Dennery Hospital and talk to the doctor. Mr Roderick tell me to give Mama's grip to the nurse and come with him. I tell him I not leaving Mama there by herself, but the nurse say is best I go with Mr Roderick and come back later after the doctor see her. I go back on the transport and Mr Roderick bring me here to the police station to call my big brother and to make a report. He tell me the doctor say I have to tell the police what I see. Miss Pinky and Mr Lucius did not come with us to the hospital; they go back to their house after they put Mama on board the van. This is my report, nobody tell me what to say."

The case I start building against Mama for not telling me the truth was nothing compared to the one I had against Papa. Corporal Jn Pierre, like Sarge, ask me to stay out of the official investigation. He promise to keep me informed, no doubt acting on the Sarge advice. He read back Marvin's statement to him after writing it over properly and ask him to sign.

Mama spend two full days in hospital; she was discharged early on the third day during the doctor's morning rounds. I find her sitting on a bench by reception waiting for Papa. She had sent a message to him through Miss Pinky who came to see her with Roderick the afternoon before. There was no taxi service from Dennery to Bwa Nèf so I had to go back to the station and ask Corporal Jn Pierre to let the driver take us when he get the chance. Mama look more frighten than frail. She did not agree with the arrangements I make so we visit my nennenn to cancel before we leave the village. My nennenn was disappointed, but Mama insist she wanted Marvin with her. We arrive at Bwa Nèf close to noon; Papa was sitting on the kitchen step pasting his shoes with Black Nugget. I didn't speak to him but overhear Mama saying: "Lovence, if I did wait for you, you want to tell me I still on the hospital bench waiting?"

"I don' own no transport; I only just get your message. Pinky leave here a minute ago." He did not seem to like Mama's tone and showed annoyance.

"Go inside and change your clothes, Mama," I urge, but she was ready for a row and pretend not to hear.

"Since last night Roderick an' Pinky pass, I tell them the doctor will discharge me in the morning. The nurse say as soon as he come. You mean to tell me is only now you get my message? Don' worry, I will ask them."

"What happen, woman, you don' well reach and you looking for trouble already, like they send you for me, or what?" He put down the shoe and the piece of cloth he was using to shine it and stare at me. "See for yourself, this is the kind of slackness I have to tolerate every goddamn day!"

I ignore him and insist Mama go inside. I follow her into the house with her little grip. I could hear Papa stomping up and down in the kitchen. "You can't stay here, Mama," I say to her. "Something bad is going to happen, I can feel it. I don't want it happening to you or Marvin. I have enough on my plate as it is."

"Nothing going to happen to me." She was confident, but I know bravado when I see it. "Lovence not himself since he come from jail. He feel ashame with everybody looking at him like is he who kill Laurette."

"What you think, Mama, he didn't do it?" I hesitate, but no, sometimes you got to be blunt.

"Why you asking me that for? You can see what I think."

"You never give a clear answer that's your problem; I have to keep asking you until I know what you mean."

"Agnes!" My father shout out from the yard. "I going down by Paulinos. When I come back I want to have a serious talk with you."

Mama crumple up like a piece of wastepaper. She open her mouth, lips trembling, going through the motions of speech without words. I hear Papa move off in a hurry, always in a hurry, that man; he didn't wait for Mama to reply, he gone. That was for the best. I crane my neck out, he was nowhere in sight. I turn to Mama hoping to talk about Papa and their life at home but she switch gears on me. "Give me some room to change my clothes; I have the man's food to cook." Already down to her petticoat, and about to pull it over her head.

I walk out of the room and went to the kitchen. There was a tin of sardines and a piece of bandja raw — that was all the food I saw. Mama put some coals in the coal pot and light a fire. I sit down watching her break some dry sticks into tiny pieces. She place the pieces crisscross between the charcoal and pour kerosene on top. Then start humming one of her hymns and carry the coal pot outside in the open to light it like she always does since I know her, when there is no rain.

Papa show no remorse. I don't know if he tell her he was sorry in their bedroom — stranger things does happen there. I don't need evidence to show his lack of sympathy; he did not disguise it. I cannot choose my father, that's my mother's job, but I can disown him, once he gives me cause. The more I thought about it, the less reason I find for Mama to continue to remain with Papa. Not because you married to him and carry his children you got to remain. It was my duty to remove Ti Frere and Mama. But where to begin? What can I say to convince her to leave? I offer to go down by Paulinos to buy some groceries for the house. Mama insisted no. "Your father will bring food when he come."

Papa did not come back until after dark, drunk, both hands swinging like police on parade. Papa march into the kitchen like a big boss. Instead of starting with the usual good night, he start harassing Mama; a strong smell of white rum on his breath full up the tiny space. He demand his food and want it warm right away. The house rule seems to me: stop what you are doing and attend to me. I wanted to ask Mama about the groceries he was supposed to buy but that would invite trouble. Shame can cause you to do and say things you don't mean, and for sure, she would feel embarrass. She dish out his food (yam and sardines) in a large bowl and place it on the kitchen table with a spoon. "Get up, Andy, an' let your father sit down." That was Mama's way ordering me out of her kitchen. She see on my face I was not pleased.

"Your father must be tired." That was a lame excuse but I got up without looking at him. Marvin bring out the old mattress he does sleep on to the front room. I was tired, and before I put my head down I fall asleep and know nothing again until fowl cock start chanting in the tall trees behind the kitchen between drizzles on the roof to tell me it going to be morning soon.

# Chapter 11

The next morning, I jump on the first minivan I meet going to Dennery and get off by the police station. Corporal Jn Pierre was off duty. I went to his house to remind him that no officer had come up to interview Mama and I was getting worried the matter was low on their agenda. I know we have a reputation for treating matters involving domestic violence cool, like they're private affairs between two people and not police business. I see a number of cases for assault, assault and battery call with neither complainant nor the accuse present on the day of the case. Perhaps this disgust officers and in the end they don't want to waste precious time on matters that will die a natural death. Corporal Jn Pierre try to reassure me this was not the case with our matter, but, he say, "Your mother has not given a statement or made a complaint. My hands are tied."

"Don't worry, I will untie them. I will bring her down to the station when you on duty."

I was suspicious about Corporal Jn Pierre. I hear rumours that he himself got a history of beating his girlfriends. He should have been made sergeant long ago but had blemishes on his file. None of the complaints he was involved in ever reach the stage to be investigated; the women withdrew before the suspect was questioned. The top brass keep him in exile in Dennery away from the bright lights.

I get back to Bwa Nèf earlier than expected. Mama was in the kitchen sitting in a corner gazing into space, both hands under her chin. I place the groceries on the kitchen table, still in plastic bags. I turn to find her eyes red, she was crying. Something happen, I hope is not another beating. She shake her head when I ask her. It's pointless quarrelling; all I could do is order her to the bedroom and put on her clothes: "We going to the station! This nonsense got to stop." I was gasping for breath, more vex than I really should.

"What nonsense?" I got her to open her mouth at last. "I go to open the window an' the wind swing it back an' hit my face."

"Which window, Mama?" She pointed to the kitchen window.

"A wind? The table is between you and the window; you either have to move the table aside or climb on it and stick your neck out. No window hit you in your face, Mama, no window gave you a black eye."

"You telling me I lie?"

"Mama don't forget my work. I solve cases worse than a black eye. I see them every day. One of these days one of you will end up dead."

"You think you know everything, eh, just because you is a policeman?" She work herself up to a frenzy using cuss words I never hear coming from her mouth before. She's repeating what she learn from Papa since he come from prison. I soothe my nerves trying to convince myself not to blame her; he put her through hell. I sit down at the kitchen table and remain quiet until she simmer down enough to listen. "Let me see your eyes, Mama," and I hold her hand. She recoiled.

"Believe what you want!" She shifted to her favourite corner, stoop down and clasp her hands between her thighs.

"Come straight, Mama, I know what happen, but you still have to say," I spoke gently.

"You come from where you come from listening to what people

by the road say and decide to make my life miserable? They tell you Lovence does beat me an' you believe them."

"Nobody has to tell me…"

"That's why you asking all these questions. I know where you going when you come up here. Some indiscreet done tell you Lovence punch me in my eye, just like they make police believe is he that kill Laurette. One of these days somebody will pay for their tongue."

"Just hope is not you, Mama." I could not resist, the remark bounce off my tongue like a sponge cake.

"Lovence never put his hand on me from the day I know him. He love me, he love Laurette, he love all his children. Tell those people that put things in your mind to leave me an' my husband alone."

"Blows not love Mama — just look at your face in the mirror."

"What you know? Is I make you, me an' Lovence and it take a lot of love to make you an' all my children." If scorn was fire, my skin would turn charcoal and burst into flames. What pass for normal in Mama's world brings hurt and pain to mine; I struggle hard to be firm: "Go, put on your clothes, I need to take you to a doctor and after that we going to the police."

"I not going nowhere. If you don' stop, I going by the road an' call your father to put you out of his house."

Stunned, no way I anticipate this. "His house, Mama?" Was all I could manage to say. This was more than a shock. "If that's what you want, I hope you find peace with yourself." I went into the house, collect my things and stand on the kitchen step fuming. "If anything happen to you don't look for help from me," I said. "It will be too late."

My heart pound inside my chest faster than a storm lambasting Dennery coast, my feet feel heavy wandering out of the yard leaving a piece of me behind. The madness around me was contagious, my mind gone crazy too. I start doubting myself asking questions I don't have answers for: what if Mama speaking the truth? What if Papa never hit her? What if everyone is lying? What if, what if? If this is love Mama, leave me and Angel as we are — I want no part in this. It take longer than usual to reach the high road, each step taking me further away from where my navel string bury, from the house that register like chapters in a book, open inside my mind; I don't want to, but compel to read it.

Mama was not living in the present, she stick somewhere else in the past when life was good and Papa was a screen star, before Marvin and me. I did not have a plan to bring her back without Papa in her life. She got to leave him, that's the only real thing for me in all of this. My conscience prick me, I want to go back to her. I stop and turn back but false pride intervene.

I plan to wait by the entrance to the gap for a van, but a breeze blow hard behind my ears and I drift lower down by Mr Paulinos instead. I might see my father; I need to say a thing or two to him before I go back to town.

Papa was there as I suspected. I hear him bragging to some friends. His voice was loud, ringing from the rafters. I catch a glimpse of him seated his back to the entrance. I don't think he see me. He had a drink or two, too many, enough to send him behaving like a politician looking for votes. I say good day to Mr Paulinos behind the bar and walk across to Papa's table in the opposite corner. "I going back to Castries," I said, without addressing him. "Before I leave, I want to have a word with you." I bend forward and speak soft in his ears. He never turn or look up, he keep staring hard at the drink in his glass on the table.

"Talk, I have no secrets, that's my friends there." He sound strange, like he didn't know who was speaking to him.

"I don't think you'll want them to hear what I got to say," I said, still soft, but he not giving in.

"Nothing you going to say they don' know already."

"You might not like what I have to say."

"Kouté gason ou!" One of his friends said but Papa insist I must talk in front of everybody — nothing I had to say was new, but I wanted it to stay private.

"OK!" I look around, measuring each face before I take a deep breath. This was going to be hard to lift off from my chest but it had to come out. "I notice you been raising your hands on Mama since you come back."

He look up at me, face sour, then raise his hand asking me to stop; it was too late. Primed and ready to go, nothing could hold me back at this stage. "I giving you a warning, take it seriously." My lips tremble, I feel them squeezing against my teeth. I never spoke like that before to him. "I am not going to say much. Make it the last time in your life you ever hit Mama, because…" I was breathless. "If you ever beat her again, I am coming back up here for you."

My voice was loud enough for everybody to hear without raising it. He did not expect me to do that. Mr Paulinos come around right away from behind the counter and stand behind me. Papa swallow the drink in his glass while his friends look on at the two of us with their mouths wide open; I turn to go.

"So, now I can't correct my wife when she do something wrong?" He laugh. "Husbands obey your wives; everything now a days back to front. I wonder who make these new rules? Before we can wink our eyes, woman will be wearing pants and we carrying the baby." If he was trying to crack a joke nobody laughed.

Mr Paulinos stand there like a referee looking confused while Papa putting on a show. It cross my mind, maybe Papa's friends does beat their wives too — that's why he was talking brave. An urge to grab him by the throat shoot through my body; pride hold me back. Things were bad, but not bad enough to fight my father in a rum shop. Mr Paulinos' firm hand grip my shoulder. "Calm yourself down, take one on me."

"Big people don't beat one another," I said, raising my voice. "Next time he touch my mother I will come up here and arrest him myself."

"Wait till the two of you get home. This is a house matter," Mr Paulinos beg me. "Your father is still your father, no matter what happen."

Papa took a penknife from his pocket pretending to clean his fingernails. Then he say. "That's why today we have no discipline. Children can say what they want to their parents and we must take it. Not me, I not going to change because the world change. I not taking shate from no child I make. I have my rules and I ready to go in my grave with them."

"Talk all you want, play big man in front your friends, but you not laying another finger on my mother again. And that's a warning in front all these witnesses here."

"Come! Come in front me if you name man and repeat what you just say." He wave the open penknife at me. To walk away would give the impression he was in charge so I laugh instead; he had the mark of a bully, something I did not notice until then.

"I'm not the same little boy in the house, the one you raise with his big sister, Laurette." I fight to drown my emotions; words don't have brakes when they in a hurry to fly out your mouth. "You can't get pass me with your hypocrisy."

"What you say?" Mentioning Laurette's name work him into a

rage. He leap out of his seat — penknife open. "I know you come for me! They send you for me! This is a set-up, but I ready for all of you!" Mr Paulinos move in between us; two of Papa's friends coax him back to his chair. I turn my back to leave without another word. Mr Paulinos follow me outside.

"Never talk to your father like that in front of people," he reprimand me. "Don't care what he do God don' like that."

"God got nothing to do with it," I snap. "Why he don't stop my father from beating Mama? He been beating her since he come from jail and nobody will stop him." I was seeing red. Oh, these people and their beliefs! Sometimes I think they have a special god make for them alone.

If I pretend those beatings Mama got did not upset my balance, I lying bold face. I was afraid to answer the phone in my cubicle at work and that fear drill deep inside, deep enough to interfere with my relations with Angel. My feelings went dead just thinking about my father and what he can do to Mama. I would curl in my corner on the bed at nights sweating while I watch Angel twist and turn in her sleep, perhaps wanting to stretch out her hand and hold me but afraid of how I will react. We barely talk during the day; only little Laurette was keeping us from falling apart.

Like Miss Beatrice, I love to relive things in the past and make vague connections where there are none. I chuckle, remembering when I start visiting Angel, things would begin nice until I reach out and try to touch her. My nickname for her was marie hont, a wild creeping plant with prickles that close its leaves like jalousies when your foot brush it. Angel would flinch. Then she hold my hand right away saying she was sorry and after give me a peck on the cheek. Angel was strange when it come to men, she could shoo them away out of her sight fast and I was real frighten she would do it to me. But with lots of patience, not rushing things and a strong will, our trust in each other blossomed.

Nothing was more disturbing to Angel than stories about men hurting women so I hesitate a little to tell her about Mama and the beatings. But then I came out with it. "What can I do? You can't talk to my mother; you can't put sense in her head. I don't understand how a woman can love a man so much that she's happy with him beating her."

"Don't try to understand. Do what you have to do to stop him, I will stand by you."

"But what can I do? How can I stop him? He's my father, I can't beat him."

"If it was me, I done do what I have to do already an' see if he wouldn't behave."

"Without a statement from Mama or a doctor's report, there's nothing I can do. She got me handcuffed with my hands behind my back."

"Until you get a call they find her dead?" The same thing again, coming from Angel it was more frightening. There was no doubt it could happen.

"But that's the law." I shrugged. "It look stupid, but that's what it is!"

"There have other things you can do; you don't have to wait for the law."

"Angel! You know I not superstitious although I was born in it. I have no faith in obeah and things like that."

She laugh and shake her head. "Is not that, Andy, I am not like my mother."

"Then what?"

"Let me go there and talk to her and you will see if she don't come down with me on the next bus to town." She raise her eyebrows like she does when she think I'm listening. "You are a policeman, use what God give you, your head!" Angel pick up the basket of dirty clothes and go outside. I play with Laurette until she fall asleep and I put her on her stomach in the cradle. I watch television until sleep take me on the chair with the remote in my hand.

# Chapter
# 12

Back at work, I continued to peruse the official dossier searching for that one clue everybody had missed. I learn techniques from television watching *Cold Case Files* and apply them where I can, but the elusive clue I was searching for could not be found — not until I speak to one of the doctors who was at Laurette's post-mortem and was able to wrap my mind around the brutality of the crime. He examined her body at the scene and at the mortuary. I read his statement many times, but to hear him repeat it was something else. I didn't understand the cold medical terms in his report but he break it down for me, sentence by sentence. I became accustom to crime scenes early — vehicular accidents on our narrow roads, witness battered bodies with open wounds, broken limbs, dismembered, lifeless — but could not relax for one minute listening to him that afternoon. My body was tense, teeth knocking as if I was inside a walk-in freezer at full blast. "The brute kill your sister then forced Gramoxone down her throat. So violent, the bottle scratched her tonsils at the back of her mouth."

Flashback to the white plastic bottle with Gramoxone. That points straight at Papa, but he wouldn't, would he? I went quiet inside. I never see Papa act violent; he never beat us. It's got to be somebody else; somebody close who know she was by Miss Claire getting her clothes hem. The crime was too brutal, too full of hate to be Papa. Conscience clash with reason inside me. What about Roderick? Fafan? Or Rupert and Curtis, that crazy couple?

Are they mad enough to commit a crime like that?

The doctor went into detail explaining how he believed the crime was committed: "The person who killed Laurette was very strong. She fought like hell for her life, clawing and biting. He did not pull, he ripped her legs wide apart with his bare hands, the ball came out from the right hip socket. It's the same male who dug his fingernail into her neck when he tightened his grip around her throat while enjoying himself. She died of asphyxia. He blocked her windpipe and starved her lungs; she couldn't breathe. She choked to death as if a piece of hard meat had stuck in her throat shutting off the air supply. If it is any consolation, you would be proud to know she did not surrender. She scratched him up left, right and centre. I found male hairs under her fingernails and they were not from his head."

I had not paid much attention to the DNA report attached to the main dossier because I did not understand it; I was better off reading Greek. However, after attending a course in Barbados and learning that DNA was more powerful than fingerprints, I begin following up on the various strides being made in the bigger countries and the positive effect DNA was having on not only arrest rates but also acquittals.

Sergeant Willius had given me permission to make copies of the official reports in my father's case files. They were handwritten and a lab technician's illegible scribble passing off for handwriting had further discouraged me from reading them. I brought the photocopies I made to a young doctor friend I know from my schooldays. He fill in the blanks for me relating every important detail in plain language. After he was finished, I had a string of questions. First one: "What part percentages play in DNA pointing to guilt or allowing for reasonable doubt?"

He didn't answer me straight but said he was happy I was

interested in the case because after seeing photographs of Laurette's body, although years later, he was sick for days. "DNA found inside your sister according to this report had deteriorated due to improper storage. Whoever was responsible kept it either out of the fridge for weeks or in a faulty refrigerator before forwarding the samples for analysis." He was as mad as me. "However, despite that, the DNA shows there is still an 85.5 per cent chance of a match with your father — this is quite high despite the condition. It could also come from a close male relative like a son, an uncle or a brother. And it also confirms Lovence St Mark is not Laurette Stephen's father." I already knew that, but it did not stop me from feeling sad.

"The test was done all the way in England. We don't have the facilities over here. Anything could happen in transit. I don't have to tell you the evidence as is also creates reasonable doubt. It could be your father; it could be his son."

"Which is me or Marvin! You have to subtract us from the equation, the two of us was still peeing in bed. Who else is left?"

"Does your father have brothers?" I could choke him for reminding me.

"Yes, but they never live with us."

"Maybe? You were too young to know for certain. All it takes is one visit."

I couldn't face my father with questions about this. I know he had brothers, two of them, but they were not close. If they ever came home, I would remember. Mama was good at family, and I could get Angel to ask her if Papa's brothers ever came home when I was small. I was desperate to find a culprit other than Papa.

Angel got a chance to talk to Mama on the phone about Papa's brothers, but she had no idea where they were. "According to Papa," she said, "one went to England and never come back and the other one I hear Lovence say was living in Castries." Imagine Mama didn't remember their names. "The brother in England been there long before your father thought of marrying and settling down," Angel informed me. "The other one learn a trade. Mama believe he was a plumber but not the kind she would ask to do work for her. He was the youngest, use to visit Papa often when Laurette was a baby because he wanted papers for an old house their mother die and leave in Praslin. After he got Papa to sign, giving away his share, he sold the house and disappeared. According to Angel, Mama said that one was a rotten egg and Papa swear he will take a dose of jail for him if he ever show his face near his house again. My mind had to move away from Papa's brothers, they could not be suspects, not by a long shot; it was not their DNA.

Then I read that the DNA results exonerated Curtis Beniot and Rupert Brown. Investigators did not find scratches on them except "superficial scars" which they got from moving about bareback under the bush. Police had to let them go. The doctor took blood and hair samples from Papa telling him it was to eliminate him and pass them on to detectives who leave the exhibits lying in a refrigerator that work when its mind tell it, until they realise their case against Curtis and Rupert was falling apart.

But why do it? My mind will not accept what may seem obvious to some people; Laurette was going to the police so he kill her to save face. That was too simple a motive to believe. Ignore, run, hide or deny, Lovence St Mark was my father and no matter what, I cannot change that fact. There was a small window of hope. I need to look deeper into the affairs of Roderick and Fafan and their links to Laurette. I should have done that long ago to see what I will find. However, with Papa's trial liable to be called at any time, I had to work extra fast. Fafan was a good candidate to work on first.

Then like a domino hand from heaven, five of the same kind with the double, I received a letter from Fafan, addressed to me care of CID headquarters. At this point I brought in Sergeant Willius and told him about my side probes. I had already spoken to five of Fafan's friends; they did not tell me much. None of them knew of anything between him and Laurette; they didn't even know that he ever spoke to her. However, they said he would skip school to go into the bush to smoke marijuana.

I question myself whether I was being fair to Fafan; I had made him a scapegoat because I wanted to believe Papa was not capable of killing Laurette. Reading his letter help me clear doubt from my mind; it was not long, but very revealing:

Dear Andrew,

I received both your letters but was worried about what to say to you without making things worse. I read where you say you investigating your sister's murder and found it strange that the case was still going on. My mother never said anything about that in her letters. As you might know Laurette hardly speak to me except for hi sometimes and she gone. After she died police came home and sit down with me and my grandmother Miss Philomene and I made a statement. They said I was the last person to see her alive, but like I did tell my grandmother I don't believe so because when I reach back that morning to get ready for school, I see her father coming from by the river where people does go to wash their clothes on Monday mornings. I did stop on my way back home to pick sugar apple. My grandmother beg me to hush my mouth or else I will find myself in trouble. This has been on my conscience eating me from that day. And after I start to work when was time for my first set of leave, I save enough money to pay for a passage to New York to get away from that place.

Please excuse me for not mentioning this until now and hope that you will be able to use it somehow to prove your case. Laurette was a nice child and did not deserve to die the way she did.

Yours truly
Fanis Jules.

After studying Fafan's letter, do I want to still find excuses for Papa? I watch Sarge while he was reading it and see a frown knot up on his face. "What you going to do?" he ask me.

"Whatever you say," I chirp back like a sikwiyé calling for his partner between a hand of ripe bananas.

The case was called twice since my father was out on bail. Each time the judge adjourn on account of some technical detail, which I never fully understand; it always had to do with lawyers wrangling over some point. I did not show interest, but inside it hurt to see what was happening in the courts with my mother having to go up and down the old road to Castries in response to false alarms. Mama stay with us each time she had to overnight. It is not an easy thing to grow up and find out the man you know as your father can commit a crime against his own family. Laurette was his child; it don't matter if her birth certificate say otherwise, or Mama say he is not. He accepted her under his roof and provide for her just like us. I know Laurette as my big sister, and nothing can change that. The pain I feel in my chest thinking about these things make me want to hate. It reach a stage where I want to see him hang for what he did to Laurette, which means is time to catch myself and move on.

All the years I spend going over evidence, it was right in front all the time as plain as a shoelace. Blaming two not so innocent lawbreakers and getting them arrested; going by Miss Claire and by the school pretending to look for Laurette without Mama asking him; not telling Miss Claire or the teacher at school Laurette missing, but going up the road to tell Mr Lucius. Fafan's letter erase what little doubt I had left. I prove my case, but not in the way I wanted. I cannot rejoice, not while Papa is still in the house beating Mama and I can't even take steps to keep him far away from her.

"You cannot leave it like that! Never know what can happen." Angel was very upset. What a wife heaven give me! I could only shake my head and hope for better times.

Angel did offer more than once to go up to Bwa Nèf and have a long chat with Mama hoping she could get her to come to her senses. However, I was surprised to come home one afternoon after six to find out she was not at home. This did not happen often, so I waited a little while until it was time to turn on the lights and call by Miss Beatrice. "Well! Well! Well! Angel is a fine one. Since morning she pick up the child and ring me to say she going in the country. She ask me not to tell you nothing, she coming back before you come from work. I hope she don' go an' give my grandchild a cold now staying out with her late in all this dew."

There was a lot of advertising on television before the news, and I was flipping through the channels: we had just bought a new colour TV on hire purchase and throw the old black and white under the house. I got up for a glass of water when I hear a key in turn in the lock. "Angel!" I call out. "What you doing out with my child at this hour?"

I could hear Angel chuckling as she open the door and pass Laurette to me well wrapped up in one of our bath towels which she had the presence of mind to take with her. "Since four o'clock I leave by your mother trying to get here before you come from work. That place behind everywhere else I know…You hungry?" She ask me as she step inside and went to light the stove without waiting for an answer.

"How was it? How's Mama?" Angel went to the fridge take out a saucepan with cow milk and put it on the fire. "I will make some tea for you and a bottle for Laurette."

"Skip the tea, unless you want. The child sleeping, you not going to wake her up now."

"When I will wake her? She hasn't ate. You want her to get up in the middle of the night hungry and bawl down the place."

I place Laurette face down in her crib and went back to Angel. "So how it went? You look quite pleased with yourself. Why you didn't tell me you were going, I would put something together for them."

"I did all of that. The reason I didn't tell you was because you would find an excuse to reach at Bwa Nèf and I wanted to spend some time alone with Miss Agnes, and I did. I am happy I went, although I can't say after all that, I understand her."

"Not in one go and you not alone in that."

"Imagine in today's world with all this internet and television there still have women who believe that after God is their man. You can see me bowing down and kiss your feet, Andy?"

"Of course, yes."

"Come off it! If I thought you would not get vex, I would say, you and your father cut from the same piece of cloth." Some things better not to hear. The milk boil over in the saucepan and Angel take it off the fire replacing it with a pot of pelau.

"Your mother is a scream," Angel giggled. "She never heard about contraceptives; can you imagine? I also mentioned tampons and she ask me what is that? Long time people really bring up their children backward, notwithstanding all those health centres with family planning and hygiene clinics all over the place."

"That's if Mama ever heard about abortion."

"Oh yes, she did. She told me about an old woman at Praslin when she was small who use to take care of the girls who find themselves in trouble with St John bush. The parish priest make the old woman's life a living hell until she disappear, nobody know where she went, but rumour had it, the devil came for her one night."

"How you expect me to sit with the two of you going through all this gossip? Tell me, learn anything new from her about Papa?"

"Humm! Now that's trouble. Every time I bring up the subject of her husband, she dodging it. The most she said was that he was a good man and she was a lucky woman to grab him when she did. One thing I can tell you her head is well screwed on. We speak about her children, she loves you all; she hasn't forgotten Laurette and swear the person who kill her will pay."

"Let's hope she don't regret that. What she said about me?"

"None of your business..."

"You spend a whole day with Mama and come back with nothing concrete, I'd call that a waste of time in my books."

"In your books, not mine. The time well spent. I get to know her and she learn me a little better. She adores little Laurette. True I didn't get anywhere with telling her that a man is not a God, and she is not his slave. She must not accept any man raising his hand on her even if he say he is her husband, that's not in any law, not in any vow she take. That did not go down well, before I could finish she start to hum a hymn for me."

I laugh so loud Angel think I was laughing at her and had to apologise. Angel set the table and dished out two plates of pelau. I forgot all about TV and the news and continued ribbing her on her failed mission until Laurette woke up and started bawling down the place, like her mother said — she was hungry.

Angel buy a cheap cell phone for Marvin to keep in touch and I call him every weekend when he was at home to find out what was happening. Every month I put ten dollars in minutes on his card and was relieved to hear Mama's voice. At least she's still alive, thank God for that! Marvin tell me Papa was not sleeping at home every night anymore, but he came on mornings to bring food; Mama still cook for him and wash and iron his clothes. Marvin said that he was out during the day looking for work and the two did not meet. He didn't know if Papa had an outside woman. More than anything else, I wanted his case heard and done with for Papa to return to jail for ten more years at least and leave Mama alone to live her life in peace. By which time Marvin would have his own family and between the two of us, we could take care of our mother comfortably.

When at last the case call Papa borrow a black suit for the occasion. I take five days off to support Mama in court. I didn't ask Angel to come. We reach early, before the usual crowd that does follow murder cases and slide into a back seat. Papa was there before us in the dock talking to a police officer, his hair sleek back looking quite unconcerned. Mama wave her hand but he never look our way.

The jurors filed in one by one, three of them was extra early like from the countryside. The registrar close to nine o'clock call out their names and remind them that they already sworn in from the previous case the evening before. However, all hell break loose when Mister Defence Attorney come in and take one look at the jurors — he would have none of it. He ask that the jury be disbanded right away and a new group empanelled. The DPP seem to agree and haggle with the registrar over a selection of eight men and four women. He push his hands in his pocket and puff out his chest: "Given the nature of this case, any good attorney worth their salt would want a balanced panel."

The judge was a woman, and the last person to come in the courtroom: "All rise." The registrar read out the case on the docket in front her and Papa's lawyer ask him to stand: "Case number 201SL12, The Crown vs Lovence St Mark, Murder."

The judge take a long look at the jury, man and woman, sizing up their clothes and then at Papa in the dock, before she glance across at the bar table. "Counsels I take it everyone one is present and ready to proceed. As I told the DPP last time, I will not entertain any further adjournments in the matter, even if Her Majesty were to come in person and demand it."

I didn't have a clue what she was taking about, maybe she was trying to make a joke. I take a deep breath when she address Papa. "Mr Lovence St Mark I see you are again represented by yet another counsel whom I assume is properly briefed. I am playing my cards close to my chest leaving no loopholes. So, let us begin. Has the jury been properly sworn in and signed?"

The registrar look like a young woman fresh out of law school. She get up and bow to the judge and hand her the book: "Yes, Milady."

Her Ladyship go through the names then spoke to the jury.

"Is anybody here related to the accused in any form or fashion?" All heads nod no. "And none of you are opposed to the death penalty either on religious grounds or on conscience, I take it."

The DPP stand up before the judge finish talking. "Yes, Mr Wilkins?"

"The jurors are properly empanelled and all pertinent questions were answered satisfactorily, Milady."

"Are you saying I am not to satisfy myself?" Look like the judge was waiting to jump on him but he stay calm and listen.

"No, Milady, far from that."

"Then, let's proceed." The judge put on her law face and read from a paper in front of her: "Mr Lovence St Mark, you stand charged of capital murder. It is alleged on Friday the 11th day of September 1998, between the hours of 8.30am and 11am in the forenoon, at Bwa Nèf in the district of Dennery in the state of Saint Lucia, you did intentionally and unlawfully cause the death of Laurette Stephen, a minor, thirteen years of age, by unlawful harm. How do you plead?"

"Milady!" The defence was on his feet. Although not a lot of people was in the hall, the place get so quiet, I feel jumpy and start to sweat. Please, not another adjournment. Mama didn't seem to follow; her eyes were only for Papa. She even mention how he looking good despite all the time he did spend in jail.

"Yes, Mr Cherris, I take it you are entering a plea of not guilty on behalf of your client, but as you may or may not be aware, I always want to hear it from the accused."

Mr Cherris hesitate a minute like the judge take the wind out from his sails. He look up at the clock behind Her Ladyship before he speak. "No, Milady, permission to approach the bench," he was already walking, the DPP behind him; Her Ladyship stop them. "What's this about? I don't like surprises."

The DPP take in front of Mr Cherris: "Milady, the matter was just discussed with me minutes before you came and although at this late hour, I believe it's worthy of consideration, because I too have my doubts."

"It better be good, Mr Watkins, it better be very good. That goes for you too, Mr Cherris — one minute."

"It's all in the line of justice, Milady…" Mr Cherris said.

"One minute! Hold your thunder for one minute."

Her ladyship seem worried. Whatever it was she was about to hear, she didn't have a clue even as she look across at the jurors. "Ladies and Gentlemen of the jury, counsel for the defence has requested a voir dire, which is a trial within a trial outside the ears of the jury. Although I haven't the slightest inkling, out of an abundance of caution I will hear him, more so as he seems to be supported by the prosecution. I will ask the sergeant to escort you to the jury room where you will remain until I send for you."

Mr Cherris and Mr Watkins take their time to approach the bench where Mr Cherris spoke first. "Milady, the prosecution and I have gone through the evidence to be presented in this case with a fine-toothed comb and we are hard-pressed to squeeze out a charge of murder from all the little strands that disconnect rather than connect a flimsy evidence. Besides most of the key witnesses are dead since this tragic incident more than fourteen years ago…"

What is this I want to scream, this case turning on its head, I hope Her Ladyship can stop it.

"Stop! Stop right now!" Mr Cherris swallowed the last word. Her Ladyship was vex; Her Ladyship was in a rage. If there was any colour for her to turn in the face it would be blue. "Why was I not informed before now of this change in plans? You know procedure, Mr Cherris, kindly explain this and explain it now!"

A humble Mr Cherris try hard to hide his skinny self in the folds of his black gown: "Apologies, Milady!"

"Had I known even at this late hour, I would have waited to hear you in chambers. The damage is done, I will deal with the two of you later in chambers. Proceed."

Mr Cherris take a deep breath, he look back at Papa and bow before he start: "Milady! The prosecution and I agree a crime was committed and for which the accused has already served fourteen years on remand and would if convicted serve more than half of a life sentence."

"That is if he was lucky to get life," Her Ladyship remark looking very irritated.

"Agreed, Milady." Mr Cherris swallow his spit. "In the circumstances my client is willing to plead to a lesser charge of manslaughter and save the court some valuable time. Especially as there is the likelihood of him being found not guilty of murder based on the evidence if this case goes to the jury in its present form."

Her Ladyship turn to Mr Watkins, I wasn't sure if she was forcing a smile or was still vex. "What say you Mr Watkins? You have been quiet all along, allowing this smooth talker to waltz me unwillingly off my feet."

Mr Watkins more shock than surprise, stammer: "My Lady, may it please the court, the elements necessary to prove a charge of murder in my opinion beyond a reasonable doubt is at best speculative…"

"Cut the fluff, Mr Watkins, such as?"

Lord, I get ready to hear English roll off the tip of the tongue between the two lawyers and know I would not be disappointed, now she is cutting them short.

"Premeditation and motive seem remote in this case. Like in

olden days, I'm being asked to make bricks without straw."

"But you are up to it, no doubt Mr Watkins, or else you would not be here." Don't mind the judge is a woman, she good for herself, I like the way she handling this case.

"Yes I am, Milady, except for that tall fence, 'beyond a reasonable doubt', I may not have legs to jump over it."

"I am in full agreement." Mr Cherris beamed. It was time for him to come out of his shell.

"You would, Mr Cherris, you would. Return to your places while I recall the jury."

The jury come in, take their seats, curious to learn what happen. Her ladyship fill them in: "During your absence counsel for the defendant and the prosecution appeared before me and were both of the opinion that there may well be insufficient evidence in this case to meet the high demands required for a capital murder conviction and I tend to agree. However, in their opinion there is enough to meet a lesser charge of manslaughter. Given that the accused is prepared to plead guilty to the lesser charge of manslaughter, your services are no longer required."

The question guilty or not guilty was again put to Papa. Mr Cherris prompted him. "Not guilty of murder, but guilty of manslaughter." Papa eat the words.

"I need to hear you!" Her Ladyship raised her voice loud. "No mumbling in my court!"

Papa bow his head and look straight at the floor, I had to strain my ears to hear him say: "Not guilty of murder; guilty of manslaughter." His complexion turn from brown to white; I sure he feel like the loneliest man in the courtroom that morning if not in the world. No sooner Papa enter the guilty plea, Her Ladyship adjourn. We would have to wait for the sentencing phase.

On my return to work Tuesday morning, Sarge was all smiles. "We got him at last; you can go and see your mother now without fear."

"Nah!" I said. "I prefer to drown myself in work." I was serious.

The detectives who work with the prosecution to bring the case to court were disappointed that all their efforts came to nothing: "The lawyers do a koko-makak between them and get the prosecutor to agree to manslaughter, a waste time," one of them said. "The man is new and not from here, he don't know the facts behind this case, they take advantage of him as a stranger." I was disheartened too. The case open my eyes to understanding this thing we call justice. Late nights at the office tidying files, putting finishing touches to some of my findings had become the order of the day for me. I was still working on the case trying to keep an open mind despite all that happened in court just to satisfy my own feelings. Angel rang me quite late one night: "When you coming home? I can't stay up forever keeping your supper warm."

We were struggling to patch things up, most of which was my fault and take the blame. To remain quiet when things happen in your family and you keep it all inside like you ashamed is not the best policy. But what else can I do? I had to spare Angel the embarrassment. Now the man is convicted, I must face the truth and get on with my life.

Angel was not the problem, it was me. I still feel raw thinking about Laurette, but I keep everything inside without talking. It never stop hurting and reach boiling point when I start hearing her voice: "He kill me an' nothing for that!" Her voice was going on and on like the alarm on a bedroom clock. With Papa entering a guilty plea, even if it was for manslaughter, guilt was guilt, but still, it can't bring relief.

Coming home on evenings I didn't feel hungry. Laurette, our

little daughter, would be asleep in her cradle while we sit by the table playing cards until late. There was no time for love, no tender words. Our relationship was turning sexless. One good thing though, we were on speaking terms. Angel keep prodding me with inquiries until I say she was invading my privacy and she get blue vex. I did not know she was afraid of losing me just like I was afraid of growing out of love. We hold on to our little Laurette like a strand of thread in a tight stitch, keeping us together, regardless.

Two weeks after Papa agree to the manslaughter plea, I was in court again listening to character witnesses his lawyer put together at short notice, including Mama. Angel leave Laurette with Miss Beatrice and come with me to the courthouse. I was happy with her sitting next to me, I felt stronger.

The witnesses painted him spotless like some saint in the church. I was tempted to get up from my seat and raise my hand, but Sarge's warnings chime in my head. "Stay out, don't get involved. Your career comes first." I watch my mother lie without blinking her eyelid on the witness stand, swearing to the judge her husband never beat her, adding: "He raise Laurette like she was his own child and she call him Papa..." I bury my face in my hands when I hear her to hold back a laugh that start deep down in my stomach. Angel thought I was crying and rub my back.

A group of prison warders, current and retired, echo Mama's music from the same hymn sheet, rehearsed, like a church choir: "He never got into scrapes; he was a good man, he never give us trouble. He keep by himself in a corner counting the days..." I never hear such bull before, how much did that cost? They said their piece and move on to the closest rum shop that I'm sure.

Papa's lawyer talk about a man I think I know when I was

small, but later turn a beast. Again, I had to squeeze the courthouse out of my mind with all this nonsense I was hearing or else I could interrupt proceedings and say my piece and get charge with contempt. I see Angel eye me sideways. She could feel I was boiling and stretch for my hand and squeeze it hard.

After everybody speak, the clerk of courts ask my father to stand. His lawyer get up too and make him a sign. The judge put on her sentencing face and address Papa: "You are a very lucky man, Mr Lovence St Mark, very lucky; indeed, it is unfortunate this matter has been dragging through the courts for more than fourteen years tying my hands. I have read all the evidence and can picture what took place. I can see this child recognising you and begging in vain for her life while you fear that she can single you out as the culprit who abused her, and for this, would you allow her to live? In fact, she must have told you to leave her alone or she will go to the police. When I consider how ferociously she fought back, I cannot believe she did not threaten you and her threat brought out the animal in you; she could not be allowed to live.

"The prosecution believes this case is short on motive, but there it is — it's all about saving face, which produced the rage that drove you to kill. Had some of the witnesses been alive to come forward to be cross-examined, you would be singing a very different tune today. I consider your actions bestial, despicable, constituting an utter betrayal of the trust this child placed in you as a parent; she even called you Papa, a name you are not worthy of. I wish I had the power to withdraw that title and privilege from you, I would gladly do it without remorse. However, justice as awkward as it seems must always be fair and balanced. Therefore, I must reluctantly agree to accept your plea of guilty of manslaughter and sentence you to time served."

The court went silent. I went cold with rage, every drop of blood in me freeze in my veins. The judge rise from her high-back leather chair and float out of the courtroom like a spider on wings. I look at Angel, she look at me, my jaw drop: "Let's go," I said. She know I done mad.

"Thank God, it's over," she replied. How she could manage to smile through all of this is beyond me. Angel wanted to say a word to Mama, at least tell her good morning, but I didn't want to force myself to say anything to my father. From where we were, I see Mama eyes fix in his direction while he was shaking hands with his lawyer and everybody else who want to show they were his friends and posing for press cameras. You would think he had been acquitted, the way he behave breaking back on the wooden bench to prop up his head and shoulders, drunk on a false air of artificial importance.

Looking at Mama adore this man got me mad. I whisper to Angel that I will wait downstairs. Not long after, I see them come down the steps, Papa holding Mama's arm, hooked to his like they were strolling down the aisle after their wedding. A reporter, camera pointing at the pappy show, stop them midway. Angel spot me in the crowd and excuse herself from the shot.

"After all this what we get is a circus," I blurt out as she come towards me.

Angel shake her head: "Andy, I know. Let's leave before you think of doing something stupid."

She cling to my arm and I feel her warm breath brush against my back. We went by her mother to pick up Laurette and remain there talking about all kinds of nonsense to take my mind off the anti-climax I never anticipate. The shock was slow to leave my system and I was glad I listen to Angel and went to the courthouse to hear for myself.

# Chapter
## 13

Weeks after the case, I finally give up on finding evidence that could point to other suspects in Laurette's murder. Papa having admitted in open court he was guilty, even if it was for manslaughter, meant there was nothing left for me to prove. The old complaint — waking up in the middle of the night breathless and sweating with my clothes damp against my skin — was back. Angel sound asleep from early — after she put Laurette face down in her cradle — curling on the pillow next to me without a clue what's passing through my mind. I jump from sleep, eardrums pounding in tune with my heart, and Mama's voice is all I am hearing: "Andy! Help me! Help me, Andy!"

Angel is alert her mother to my situation. A new lamp appear on the shelf in our bedroom that afternoon; Miss Beatrice insist is a kòkma that hold me in its clutches and push Angel to buy a new one. By an unexplainable mixture of events, the dreams stop. I start going to the gym every day and this help clear my mind. Angel was happy and we settle down planning an extension to the family.

One morning not long after Papa was released, fighting off a last-minute sleep before I get up to pee, my cell phone ring. I answer soft: "Hello!" watching Angel stir, irritated by the noise; I start to shake before I hear who is at the other end.

"Is me." I recognise the voice, gruff and breaking into a man.

"Marvin? That's you?" Everything fly out my head even sleep. "What happen now, you calling me so early, something happen?"

The answer take forever to come. "Since last night I calling you!"

I was ice-cold, breathing heavy. "Don't tell me is Papa again!" I check Angel and see her turn and stretch with one eye open.

"Who's that?" she ask sitting up.

"It's Marvin! Shush!"

"Papa beat Mama again!" Angel exclaims, enraged sitting up.

"When I couldn't get you, I call the police," Marvin said. "He's in the cell at Dennery Police Station. He say when he come back he putting me out of his house because I supporting Mama in her nonsense." Marvin was panting.

"Nonsense like what?" The line start cracking, Marvin's voice fade, I could barely hear against the background static.

"My father again," I said to Angel. "This time police have him."

"It must be real bad! You want me to come with you?" She got out of bed and went to the toilet. "It have to stop, Andy!" Angel shouted through the half-opened door. "This thing about man beating woman and getting away scot-free not in my books!"

When I got to work, Sergeant Willius tell me several times he was fed up with Lovence St Mark and was coming with me to put an end to his nonsense once and for all. On this occasion, he swear to arrest Mama if she refuse to talk and don't care what I say or do. He call Dennery Station for a status report on the investigation, but Corporal Jn Pierre was not at work yet. Sarge record in the logbook: "Out with Private Andrew Stephen investigating a complaint. A serious case of assault and battery at Bwa Nèf Dennery. Suspect in custody."

By the time we reach Dennery, Corporal Jn Pierre was there. Nothing happen overnight, except the officer on duty earlier had released my father before leaving without consulting his superior officer. Jn Pierre said the man only beat his wife and he didn't see anything seriously wrong to keep him from earning a day's pay and enter his reason for the release in the log. Sarge lose his cool; the veins in his neck dance a mad débot as blood rush to his head. "The officer acted outside of his authority." You'd think they were going to fight. "How you can let this happen on your watch; summons that private back here, right now!"

Sergeant Willius requested transport to go to Bwa Nèf; he insist on finding my father. "I need to give him a serious warning and if I get any back chat, I'm returning him to the cell."

"You can't ask the man to stay away from his wife without a court order," Corporal Jn Pierre advised.

"He wouldn't know that. Send the driver with us as soon as he gets back from delivering summons. I know you fellas must protect your bad habits. I also know the loopholes in the law to exploit."

Meanwhile, I was calling my brother until my fingertips get numb; his cell stop ringing for good. That don't look right, I tell myself. Sarge seem to overhear and take a long hard look at me. "Call him again 'til he answer." Sarge baffled like me tried to grasp what was happening. "Maybe his phone stop working, or he take out the battery." He snatched the phone from me and request the number.

Sarge hold the phone outside the window and dial. "It's ringing," he said and pass it back. I place it to my ears; it went dead.

"Bad connection." I dial the number again and listen. "Sarge, the damn thing ringing but he not answering!"

"Could be where he is. Call him again when we get closer."

The road had got worse since I last go up to Bwa Nèf. We were in the rainy season and there were potholes everywhere; drains overflow and run across the road. The driver took his time in and out of deep crevices. I check my watch over and over the minute we turn off the main highway. We reach Bwa Nèf after ten. Sarge ask the driver to remain with the vehicle by the road but tell him he could relax a little, go down by Paulinos' rum shop and wait for us there. The driver lick his lips and smile; I didn't hear what he say.

We follow the dirt track, large enough for bicycles but not jeeps. When we reach Ma Philomene's old house, Miss Pinky was in the window waiting; maybe somebody had run ahead to tell her to expect us. Who say news never travel fast under the bush; if you don't watch yourself, it faster than telephones.

"Morning Miss Pinky, how things?" I give her a shout. "How's Ma Philomene?"

"My mudder dere lying down on de bed waiting on de big boss to call her name, you know already."

"When last you see my people?"

"Not for dis morning as yet." I notice she was cheerful, but not after she see Sergeant Willius with me. "Someting happen? Someting got to happen, since when you coming here with police..."

"Nothing much Miss Pinky, we just passing through."

"Let me put on my clothes. Tell Agnes I coming up dere now."

"Ask her if she hear any noise during the night," Sarge whisper. Miss Pinky didn't need me to repeat, her ears were razor sharp.

"Last night I hear dem quarrelling, but dey always quarrelling; I see Lovence pass down as usual an' go by the road, I don' see when he pass back; it was too dark."

"You see anybody this morning?" Sarge asked.

"Noooh!" Miss Pinky answer, her curiosity juices were bubbling over. "Someting happening?"

"We in the area doing some routine checks, I decide to check up on home." I sound more worried than casual which send Miss Pinky to start guessing.

"Somebody sick?" I sense an edge in her voice.

"No! Nothing like that," I answer. As we begin to climb the hill towards the house, I take out my cell phone and called Marvin again. From where we were, we could hear his cell phone ringing, the sound was coming from the kitchen. Although separated by bush, we were close. Sarge who have experience of such situations shake his head. "That's not good."

We rush up the little hill, faster than I ever climb it. My cell cut off and the ringing stop. I knock on the side of the kitchen near the window, which open in the direction of the main road and shout: "Marvin, why you not answering your cell?" No answer.

The air around me was thick against my skin, the place quiet, I could almost touch the silence. Sarge creep ahead to the edge of the kitchen and craned his neck into the yard. He turn in slow motion, then raised both hands: "Stop! Don't come any further! You have your piece?" What I need a gun for? I said to myself. My mind get knotted in vines. I believe I shout, "No." Why take a gun to come and talk to my father? Sarge hadn't taken his gun either. However, from where I was, I could see like something hit him hard across the face; I paralyse too. My feet, my hands, anchor me where I am standing. I can't shift left, can't move right. I see the tail of his shirt jack head towards the kitchen steps moving very slow on tiptoe — he didn't want to mash the ground too hard in case it disappear under his foot.

Somehow, I inch forward ignoring his orders. I could see the open back door, the bedroom, but not the whole yard. My head start to spin. I didn't notice Miss Pinky shoot pass and begin bawling down the place as if her mother finally decide to go.

"I tell you to stay where you are!" I hear Sarge voice but couldn't see him. Miss Pinky was in the middle of a fit, screaming and pulling out the little hair left on her head.

"You messing up a crime scene!" Sarge was speaking to Miss Pinky. I could now see Miss Pinky holding Mama by the shoulders and shaking her hard. Mama was sitting on the kitchen steps holding a body across her lap. From the feet, shoes and pants, it was a man; it's Papa. But things take a while to register as if I in the cinema watching in slow motion. I could see blood, lots of blood. I go from feeling giddy to feeling numb. Sarge try to stop me; I was too strong for him. I pull Miss Pinky away from Mama and she grabbed me by my neck. I was taller than her and could see over her shoulder. Mama's eyes were wide open gazing past us, staring like a statue into space, face blank, eyes dry, she was not crying, not even vex. She hold on to Papa tight like a baby and would not let go. I could see his head was not where it was supposed to be but I was too dazed to absorb what I was seeing, too numb to react. "Mama! Where's Marvin?" The only conscious thought that came to me. I bawl at her, loud.

"He's not here," Sarge said.

Blood was all over Papa's clothes, I couldn't tell the colour of his shirt; I couldn't tell the colour of Mama's dress either — her hands, her neck, her legs, all red.

"Hold her!" Sarge shouted. "I have to secure the yard before people start coming and trample up the place."

Hold who? I believe he mean hold on to Miss Pinky as she was the only one moving about. Sarge jump over Mama and climb into the kitchen. He finds a brace of rope and Marvin's cell phone. He ask me if I recognise the phone; it was the same one Angel buy for Marvin.

Conscious, yet unconscious, I watch Sarge tie one end of the rope to a nail on the side of the kitchen, the other end to the corner of the house. People would hear Miss Pinky scream and come running into the yard, ears are sharp in this part of the woods. Sarge got on his cell to headquarters. I hear him ask to notify Dennery Station. Don't ask how but I manage to get Miss Pinky to sit down by the bedroom door. I try to take Papa out of Mama's hands, but she double over and wouldn't let me touch his body. Sarge plead with me to leave her alone. "CID on their way."

I remember sitting down by Miss Pinky and looking across at Mama on the kitchen steps. "What happen, Mama? What happen?" Is all I remember saying and looking at all the blood splattered everywhere just shaking my head over and over.

# Chapter
## 14

I was twenty-five and think I see everything in life, but until that moment I hadn't seen anything at all. Nothing so far to prepare me for what we find. I can't explain the shock, the suddenness of the situation.

I still feel paralysed when I think about that morning. Writing this after the fact, sends a chill through my bones. I still see Papa's head hanging by string of flesh to his neck and that makes my skin quail like bird meat. From that day I lose my appetite for pork. The bleeding stopped before we got there, but his eyes, like two crystal marbles, wide open, bloodshot red; I can't forget that picture. I climb over Mama into the kitchen, take a large cup, fill it with pipe water and give Miss Pinky to wash the blood from her hands and face — nothing could be done about the mess she made with her clothes. Miss Pinky revived after washing her face but was still shaky.

After she tidy up a little, she sit down with Mama until the Flying Squad arrive. They came from Vieux Fort and reach before the CID officers, who were coming all the way from Castries. In the confusion, we forget the driver by the road and had to ask one of the Flying Squad officers to inform him. I keep asking Mama for Marvin. Where was he? The silence in the yard catch Miss Pinky unawares, and she and Mama sit in the kitchen doorway, faces blank, staring at the old house facing them.

Frustrated, not having the facts and with nobody to explain what happened, I start patrolling the place like I on the beat while Sarge go about doing his work securing the scene. Then I remember Angel and call but couldn't reach her and that had me more mess up. Sarge ask me to please leave everything as is and sit down quietly and wait. I obey.

When CID arrived with a full squad, uncovering everything, searching everywhere, taking photographs of Papa's body, Mama still in her bloodstain dress, Miss Pinky, the kitchen, the house, the yard; they fill their paper bags with evidence. An officer find a four-nail cutlass with blood on the blade in the bush behind the kitchen.

It was hell to get Mama to give up Papa's body after the doctor arrive. The men from the undertaker, who were on the scene together with CID, went to great lengths to take Papa's torso out of her hands. On information passed on by the Flying Squad, CID knew Papa was already dead and saved the ambulance a useless trip. The doctor confirm they were right. My one consolation, Sarge was in charge; I would get to know everything and that cool me down a little

Don't mind what I think about Papa, or what I tell Mama about her husband; don't matter I reject his surname for Mama's and want to see him pay for Laurette's murder, now he's dead, I want to know who kill him. I cannot be on the investigating team, family is not allowed, but I can help. I follow Sarge everywhere watching him pass on instructions, saying what to look for and what to bag. The doctor take a long look at Papa's neck and in my presence announce, "Death was caused by a single blow from an extra sharp instrument like a cutlass." He took the body temperature. Papa was still warm. He concluded that Papa died less than four hours before he examined the body.

Sarge ask Miss Pinky to take my mother and change her clothes; he needed her dress as evidence. She would also have to accompany him down to headquarters. The doctor calm her with an injection; Miss Pinky collect water from the standpipe in a white enamel basin from the bedroom and rush back inside.

I ask Sarge privately if he think Mama is a suspect. "Everybody in the house is a suspect for now. We have to find your brother and fast."

Despite my training, it was hard to admit that Marvin was the prime suspect. I forget he was not like me that grow up with Papa in the house. Marvin only get to know him when he come from jail, but still that didn't disqualify Lovence from being his father. The cloud on my brain start to thin out and things begin getting clearer as people start arriving in small groups. Word made the rounds from mouth to mouth around Bwa Nèf, up Tèt Chimen, into Gwan Bwa.

The Flying Squad was having their hands full keeping busybodies behind the barricades and fielding all kinds of questions floating through the air. Sarge speak to them, inquiring about my brother; asking if anyone had seen him that morning. I could hear them mumbling; they want to be part of the excitement with nothing to say to police. Nobody saw Marvin, he did not pass near their house, he was not by the high road, they did not meet him under the bush…Whether or not the information was true was another matter. They whisper aloud about Papa; none had anything good to say about him but doubt Marvin killed him. "He get what he sow, he paying for his sins and what he do to his child." This was the consensus among Bwa Nèf people. Their minds were made up and nothing on God's good earth would change their point of view.

Mama put on the same clothes she wear whenever she go to Castries; it was like the *onliest* dress in her wardrobe good enough for these occasions; she believe it make her look presentable. She walk out and stand in the yard like she didn't know where she was, staring at the crowd behind the police yellow tape as if asking herself what all these people doing there. Miss Pinky offer to stay back and clean after the police leave. Mama remain blank; she didn't seem to understand. On our long journey to Castries, Mama sit in the back of the vehicle all the way without saying a word, her eyes were dry, not a bead of sweat on her forehead although the jeep was not air-condition. At headquarters, I was glad to find Angel waiting. How she get to know, I didn't ask her but I suspect Corporal Jn Pierre from Dennery station call her.

Angel invite Mama to stay with us until she feel strong enough to go back to her house. Two days after Papa's death the shock start to wear off. On the third day, Mama's mind appear to settle; she ask Angel about our plans for Papa's funeral. She help Angel bathe Laurette and played with her for most of the day. The change in her spirit was magic.

The doctor write in his statement on the postmortem: "Judging by the blood spatter on his wife's clothes, she held her husband while he was still alive." Doc did not elaborate, but when I met him in private, he said: "It is not easy to witness a death violent like that one; it does things to your psyche. People go mad when faced with less. She is not normal so don't press her."

I make all the arrangements for the funeral after the postmortem was complete and bury my father in Dennery exactly one week after finding him dead. Mama wanted him buried at Bwa Nèf, next to Laurette; I say no and stand up to her. She got me very angry: Mama might be Lovence wife but burying him next to Laurette was not going to happen not while I and Angel was spending our money.

After the funeral, Mama say she want to go home so I went up to Bwa Nèf and spend the night with her. Angel went back to town to take care of Laurette. Next morning while getting ready to leave, Miss Pinky, Miss Claire and Mr Lucius come to the house with Mr Paulinos; some other people I did not know came with them. They came to cook and prepare for the eight nights' wake. They bring their food, ground provisions, frozen chicken and plenty of drinks. They put everything on the kitchen table and take over the whole place. Miss Claire ask Mama if she hear from Marvin and tears (as usual) come from her eyes and couldn't stop. I beg Miss Claire to be careful talking to Mama. I assure her police was out in numbers looking for Marvin and they would soon find him. Mr Lucius overhear and join the conversation: "What there to happen will happen, we can' stop that. None of us bigger than God." The holiness in this place will kill me if I come back to live here.

Everybody around, except Mama, tune in adding their grain of salt. They insist Marvin could not be the killer; he see everything and hiding, afraid for his life, because the killer know he see him. Few believe Marvin was still around under the bush. They were careful not to blame anybody or mention names, keeping their suspicions to themselves. Some believed Marvin go and meet his ex-schoolmates in Dennery and they were hiding him from police. "If that's the case, why police up here searching, they will never find him like that," Miss Pinky spoke loud; the gossip was getting to her head. I ask Miss Pinky to take care of Mama while I go back to Castries and I promise her to return in time for the wake. I leave mid-morning and arrive before noon. Sarge give me a little briefing; he suspect certain individuals at Bwa Nèf were feeding Marvin. I ask who. He smile and said no more.

After eight days with patrols falling over each other under the bush, there was no trace of Marvin anywhere, not even footprints. If he was getting help, I was sure Mama would know; however Angel insist I don't mention anything about that to her.

I remember Roderick — he never like Papa, and there were more like him at Bwa Nèf. My conscience prick but said nothing to Sarge. Detectives ran a dragnet and round up Marvin's friends and old schoolmates in Dennery village; all claim they hadn't seen or heard from him. I worried sick, afraid he was dead. He not soukouyan that appear and disappear when they want or walk on the ground without leaving a mark. Marvin can't be still alive and nowhere to be found. Perhaps the person that kill Papa, kill him too, to make sure he keep his mouth shut and bury him in a place hard to find. The boy is almost eighteen, but don't know how to survive in the forest, how to fight the dew and cold under the bush at night. What does he know about snake bite?

Strange ideas keep coming and going. Is Marvin responsible? Is he on the run? Why? Why Mama not speaking? When things don't fit in place suspicion provide you with ideas. Nothing about Marvin's disappearance make sense, unless he did it. If he didn't do it, why hide? There was a witness, blood splatter on her clothes tell us that. If Mama would only come out and talk I would stop worrying. However, it's not easy to get her to break her silence. I lose my sister, then my father — doesn't matter what I believe about him — now I going to lose my brother too.

I hire a car for the night; Angel and Sarge come with me to the wake. Angel decide she shouldn't leave me to take the strain alone. "Here's two hundred dollars," she said. "Don't lose it; death don't come cheap." She hand me a sealed envelope and ask me to give it to Mama. She was particular to remind me, it was her own money.

Sarge insist we need company on the way back. The moon was out from seven o'clock, nice big full moon. Everybody was in the yard giving jokes and carrying on like every other wake. Mama remain in her room; Angel stay with her. She ask about the baby — Angel told me after — like she forgot her name, or was afraid to mention it. They talk about me, things that happen when I was small; Angel was inquisitive and want to know how I behave as a child, and all other kinds of maji I get involve in. She help Mama to come out of her shell and loosen up. Angel knew about Mama's clash with high blood pressure, which come after Papa return home on bail, and tried hard to get her to relax and remain calm. However, when Angel thought she was succeeding, Mama clamp shut again, hands trembling like she remember something that change her mood; it take a small shot of white and a glass of water to calm her down. Miss Pinky join Angel in the bedroom and together put Mama to bed like she was a baby and stay until she fall asleep.

Sarge and I partner against Mr Paulinos and Mr Lucius in a game of dominoes outside and get beaten badly. Sarge was more interested in Marvin than in the game and was asking questions in between moves. I ask to be excused and went behind the kitchen to relieve myself. While there with my mind in some other place, I hear a voice like a boy pretending to play he's a man: "Frere, is me!" It was a gruff whisper. One time, pee stop; I fix myself in a hurry, you'd swear (if you see me) I was embarrassed as if somebody catch me urinating in public. I look where I hear the voice coming from and see nothing but black. Then moonlight was pouring through the trees; my eyes could see shapes. The breaking voice, I hear it again: "Frere, Andy, I couldn't take it; it was too much."

My eyes gradually get accustom to the dark, and I see Marvin appear from behind the shadow of a mango tree. Moonlight escape between some branches. He was wearing khaki long pants and a short-sleeve white shirt. In the faint light dripping through the leaves, he did not resemble somebody who been hiding for more than a week. His clothes look clean. His face smooth, no sign of overnight stubs under his chin. "I want to give myself up, but I afraid police beat me."

"Beat you for what? You kill Papa?"

I could see the white in his eyes; my eyes were still good; they train under a kerosene lamp; he was looking straight at me.

"Poor Mama, she couldn't take any more blows from him. I had to stop Papa or else he would kill her…" His voice drop.

"No police will beat you for that."

"After all the trouble I give them, they still looking for me."

"As far as I know, you didn't kill an officer…"

"What about Mama? She will be against me; I sure she hate me."

"We don't know that. Up to now she hasn't said a thing, neither to me or police."

"If you know they will not beat me, I want you to take me to the station yourself."

"Sarge is there with me, he's in charge. We will take you in together."

"Don't tell him what I tell you."

"That you kill Papa?"

"Don't tell him! That's between us, OK Andy?"

"OK, I will not tell him. Wait for me here, I will go and call him."

"Why?"

"You say you want to give yourself up."

"Yes, but you don't have to call him now."

"Marvin, what you want to do?"

"I tell you already."

"Well, go back in the bush and wait."

Marvin disappeared in the shadow of the mango tree. I walked back to the yard where I left Sarge at the domino table.

"That was a long pee." He look up at me. I made him a sign to follow me. "Marvin want to turn himself in," I whisper, making sure nobody else hear.

"I suspect he would come to the wake," Sarge grinned. The moonlight was shining bright in the yard. "Where's he?"

"Marvin!" I call out without raising my voice. I hear something tickle a leaf and run up a branch, must be a manicou, they out at night creating havoc. I leave Sarge leaning against the old kitchen and went into the bush exactly where I saw Marvin disappear. "He would go and hide until I come back."

"Careful!" Sarge warn me loud.

"It's OK, he's my brother."

Further into the bush, a thick branch block most of the moonlight from piercing through the leaves above my head. I didn't have a torchlight and couldn't see past the next tree. I walk blind between trees calling Marvin, not loud, loud, but enough for him to hear. I walk until my eyes get familiar with things around in the darkness again, but there was no sign of him. I hear a voice behind me say: "He's gone." It was Sarge, he follow me and I didn't know.

"Maybe he didn't want people at the wake to see him," Sarge said. "Shame can make a man do things he don't want to do." I didn't understand what he was trying to say. Marvin say he want to give himself up so why would he say that and disappear? My mind was up to its old tricks, I keep myself questioning myself if I gone crazy. Did I really see Marvin? Did he speak to me?

What's Sarge thinking? He must be saying I gone off for real this time.

We give up and return to the domino table. Mr Lucius ask if anything was wrong. Sarge answer him no. Neither Mr Lucius nor Mr Paulinos prolong the conversation; they concentrate on their game without blinking an eyelid as if they know something and was laughing inside at us. I did not mention anything to Mama to cause another disaster and a fresh round of tears. We leave for Castries fore day morning. Sarge drive all the way back and drop Angel and me by our house. He keep the car until he come to work later that morning and I turn it in.

A policeman's job is tough, but when you are a detective and family is involved in matters being investigated by your department, it gets tougher. First, my father was on trial for the murder of my sister, now it's my brother who disappear and we searching all over this little island for him in connection with Papa's death. Oh God! You not kind to me. Don't tell me that Mama and me going to be on the road up and down until this case call. Not another fourteen years again. What a life! Heaven help me, please!

Every time reports come in I'm on edge. Officers notice this and keep information away from me. Some believe I know more than I am saying, others show sympathy but very little else. Sarge, on occasions, out of the blue sky does ask if I hear from Marvin, pretending it's routine, off the cuff, absentminded, but I know better. I would do the same thing if I was in his place. I trust him enough with the truth if I get to hear anything, but not Mama, she didn't trust us.

She maintain her silence on Papa's homicide despite investigators confronting her with evidence which show she was present on the scene and witness everything: the soiled dress, the amount of blood, the thickness on her clothes, the blood splatter on her face and the kitchen. Grilled by the top brass, accused as accomplice, threatened with harbouring a fugitive, nothing the big boys throw at her could break Mama; she gave no information, good or bad about Marvin. It was as if he never was born — she didn't know him.

The blood on the cutlass behind the kitchen match Papa's but the fingerprints on the handle were not Mama's and that help clear her as a suspect. As a woman always suspicious of strangers, Mama keep to herself in her little house on the hill but could not stop casual visitors dropping by unexpected. They came with one purpose in mind and would show their badges before annoying her with questions about Marvin and Papa. This went on for months until she start coming to herself and plant a little garden behind the kitchen to occupy herself.

Angel would buy groceries once a week and send for her. We tried to visit once a month but that did not always work out. Nevertheless, our visits came like duty especially when the weather was good enough to bring Laurette. One thing took a long time to understand and puzzled me — because Mama never does anything without a reason. She keeps asking about Marvin's cell phone; it couldn't be that Mama got sentimental overnight. Every time she asked I tell her the same thing, Marvin's phone is evidence but that didn't stop her asking again next time I come. I mention it to Angel, and she wondered if Mama simply needed a next phone. I offer to buy one for her, she insist no. Aware of Mama's strange habits, I let the matter rest. Nevertheless, she asked again and again, every trip. "When I going to get Marvin's phone?"

My visits to Mama get me unpopular in the force with my friends, especially the detectives working Papa's case, including close ones like Corporal Jn Pierre, and, in a way, Sarge although he had no direct involvement. Nothing could convince them that I knew nothing about my little brother and his whereabouts. Once or twice the chief ask me direct and showed surprise when I say I couldn't help him.

The police suspected Mama was in contact with Marvin and believe I knew. "They not telling you what they know, they staying far, hoping you'll make a mistake. They watching you twenty-four seven, want to bet?" Angel said. I learn to never take bets with Angel. She does not lose. I beg her to go to the country without me and find out what's going on. If anyone could pick Mama's tongue it was her. Angel look at me and screw up her face in a way that say that she's not doing that and get cold with me for not being fair to Mama. "What you think Marvin not her child too? She didn't suffer to make him the same way she make you?"

Don't ask me how she arrive at that, but I think it's the old story of a policeman taking an oath to arrest his mother, which she believes as a matter of fact. "You on the same side with the police and forget Miss Agnes is your mother."

The last thing I want was for Angel to give me the cold shoulder. If Mama say something to me in confidence, I don't think I would repeat it to anybody. Angel does not believe me. I wake up nights trying out several situations dealing with Marvin's disappearance and each one lead back to Mama. Her silence, the blood spatter on her dress, Papa's body in her arms like a baby, Marvin's appearance the night of the wake, his clean clothes, clean face — I don't have to ask and she don't have to say a thing, Mama have a big hand in that. Angel and I debate the facts between us, by involving her and talking frankly, help diffuse any growing resentment between us that involve Mama.

Sarge, although not with me like before, never tell anyone, or make an entry in the case file that I was in contact with Marvin at Papa's eight nights' wake. Even so, all of this tell me that I would not get promoted in a hurry: too many disasters in my family, which make me appear uncooperative to the top brass in the force. I discuss my fears with Angel; it was clear I would go nowhere. So when I got offered a job with a private security firm that had contracts with big hotels on the island, I took it. They hire me as an instructor and send me on a three-month course to Jamaica for special training. By that time Angel was having our second child, with two mothers to pamper her during pregnancy, mine and hers. When I return Angel was waiting for me, ready to give birth.

There was still no word about my brother. Sarge told me they gave up searching for him. The case had already turned cold on some young recruit's desk. Somewhere in my head Marvin ship out on a boat; there was a lot of people from Bwa Nèf and Dennery village willing to help him and told me so without asking. Rumours that he was in St Vincent was never confirmed, nor in Trinidad. And those with guts lie to police insisting he was a pork-knocker in Guyana, mining for diamonds.

Knowing the closeness between Angel and Mama, I never attempt to ask her if Marvin does write his mother. I did not want to look like I was digging although I was no longer a policeman, I know the kind of cut eye I would get. Mama never mention Marvin in any of our conversations, neither Laurette nor Papa. You'd think she erase them from her life. Angel swear she was doing her best to squeeze the facts from Mama about the morning Papa bleed to death in her hands. She was curious after all this time why Mama never feel like clearing her conscience: "All she doing is smile for me when I ask her, a smile that not stopping until I stop asking her questions." What Mama know, I assume will go to the grave with her and switch off from everything that have to do with Papa's death. It was no longer on my chest.

After I took up my new job, I married Angel and our second child was born, a son, we name him after my friend, Sarge, because without him, I would not last a fortnight at CID with all those sharks out for a piece of my clothes. I was adjusting to civilian life, and the new experience of being a married man, when, within a space of minutes, two phone calls from CID would shake my peace. First to call was Sarge to say he coming over by me. The other call came from Sergeant Jn Pierre recently promoted after marrying his child mother and transferred to Castries. "Marvin give himself up to immigration at the airport."

I tell Angel what happen and I ask her to contact Mama before she get the news from strangers. Sergeant Jn Pierre promise to let me know when Marvin was brought to the station so I can come down. Before he call back, Sarge, who was now Inspector Willius, came by me to tell me that he received a call from the Chief Immigration Officer that a man with a Guyana passport came in on a flight from Barbados saying he was Marvin St Mark and wanted to surrender to him. "I wasn't sure, so I don' call you right away. I instruct immigration to detain him until I arrive. If I tell you the young man is the picture of you, wait till you see him cause you will not believe me. His documents, excellent forgeries, I haven't seen better, down to the ID card he was carrying; it must be cost a small fortune to buy that. I didn't know he knows me that well and recognise me the moment I reach, he even address me as Sarge."

Angel sit down next to me breastfeeding the baby, listening quietly. Every time I get anxious and want to interrupt, I can feel her holding me back. Sarge get more work up as he speak, "Marvin said he did it, he kill his father. I now have the headache to put the evidence together and make sure he can get a speedy trial."

It was my turn to interrupt, Angel or no Angel. "How much time you got left in the force again?"

"Next year I will be fifty-five, retirement due, but if they want me they will hold me till sixty."

"I not counting on that."

"What?" Angel asked. "I don't follow."

"The old problem, postponement after postponement staring at me in the face," I said to her.

"This case not calling today or tomorrow, CID will want to go over every inch of evidence before passing the file on to the DPP. I can't forget what they do to Papa, and they still bear a grudge against me, they think that I let Marvin escape."

"You might be right with everybody looking for promotion," Sarge said.

The gleam in Angel's eyes go out as she get up to put the baby to sleep and come back for Laurette. Sarge was not looking normal, and I didn't have to guess that, like me, he was doubtful that even with a guilty plea things would flow normal. "I think I will wait for Mama to come down and we will come to the station together in the morning. I don't want raising suspicions."

"I will hold him at CID. Come after nine."

It was near to midnight when Sarge left. Neither Angel or me wanted to sleep, we were excited that Marvin was alive and Agnes would be seeing her son again. I notice, however, after a while Angel got silent but started following me around with her eyes. I went to the toilet, brushed my teeth, came back and put on my pyjamas but her eyes were still following me.

"He should have stayed where he was," Angel squeaked. "Not come back here to give us this kind of trouble, the going up and down almost kill Mama. Hmmm, I wonder what your mother will say after she see her son?"

"Worry for yourself, not for her."

Angel sized me up sideways. I could feel she wanted to tell me something but didn't know where to start, and she bit her lip more than once before I asked her what it was.

"Not today, I wanted to tell you something, but I didn't know where to start."

"What! You got a spare man on the side?"

Her eyes laughed, seeing I could still crack a joke despite the pressure on me and her tongue untied. "You remember I give you an envelope for your mother and tell you it had two hundred dollars to help her with the wake?"

"You think I have that studying; what I want to remember that for. You give my mother two hundred dollars, so what, that was so long ago. You want the money back?"

"No, Andy." Angel gave me one of her special smiles that could turn my insides to jello and I stretched out to embrace her but she slipped out of my hands. I followed her into the bedroom and sat down with her on her side of the bed. Angel rest her head on my chest and held my hand without looking at me in the face. "You know I will never lie to you just so…"

"Yea! Where's all this coming from? You of all people should know never get a detective suspicious."

"An ex-detective, correction!" She laughed and lifted herself to her feet and turned facing me squarely. "Well I lied. When I told you I gave Mama two hundred dollars, it was nine hundred, and before you start helling and damning I will do it again for her if I have cause."

In that mood Angel is a rebel best left alone, next she will be quick to say it was her money not mine. She looked at me eyes wide, staring. "I couldn't tell you the truth what the money was for, so I made up something."

"Not another word, I don't want to know. Let me suspect. That lodge Mama and you join don't need me around to interfere."

Only then I realise there had been tension between us while Sarge was at home, Angel might have been feeling the full brunt of it under the guilty shadow of suspicion. She was not aware of how much Marvin had said to him, a good officer never gives details. This must have also given her the courage to talk. How many sleepless night she fretted over this, poor soul? A strange sensation took over my feelings; it was not guilt. I asked myself what I would have done had I known the truth but couldn't think hard enough to surface with an answer. Marvin had surrendered to police and that was enough for me.

Angel got hold of Mama and they spoke for a long time on the phone. Afterwards she shared another secret with me, one that puzzled me from soon after Papa died and Marvin disappeared. "Strange you don't ask me why Mama was always asking for Marvin's phone."

"That's one mystery I forgot. Didn't even realise she stop asking."

"Well, I asked her. She tell Marvin was absentminded and was afraid he call his number by mistake while the phone in police hands."

"Who say Mama not smart," I shout out loud and reached for Angel lying on the bed next to me and hugged her tight.

I meet Mama by Dennery bus stand a little after eight next morning. We went up the road together to the Serious Crimes Unit, where Inspector Willius arrange for us to see Marvin alone.

For me, I feel nothing when I see my brother again at the station. It was as if in the company of a stranger but Mama held on to him tight like Papa after he was dead. To me it seemed Marvin had taken Papa's place. Nothing about Marvin looked like a fugitive, a full-set man, coarse voice, huge biceps, and a large neck, had to be doing heavy-duty work as far as I can observe. "When I come to understand everything that happen was heavy on my conscience, I had to stop hiding."

I didn't ask him questions; I wasn't too sure what to ask, but he was opening up to me. I recognise I was under a spell, probably in shock. My little brother — although he didn't look so anymore — in custody admitting to killing our father is not something you take with a grain of salt. Mama talk about getting him a good lawyer, but never ask him one question about where he been all this time, which confirmed to me, she knew. Deep inside I cared and I worried about the long wait for Marvin's day in court what it will do to Mama and Angel, and to Angel and me. However, on account of our two small children I had to borrow a hard face. They do not carry the surname St Mark, I make sure of that. Yet still we are one family and regardless of what comes next, we will all stand together behind Marvin, until we can get him acquitted of whatever he was supposed to have done — though I suspect our Laurette will be an old woman by then. With Angel and Mama in partnership, heaven help who get stuck in between.

I hear church bells chiming in my head, not Easter, not Christmas, it's the middle of the week. Must be my big sister celebrating in heaven. In the end, she wins; justice for her of the purest kind has won. From here Mama and me will pass in the cathedral and light a candle for her at the feet of Our Lady, patron of all hopeless causes.